SERGEANT MA
Space Soldier

BY G.H. White

DEDICATION:

I offer special thanks to my wife, Michelle, and our friend Mary Ann Dority. Their efforts made the book more readable for any reader.

A special thanks to Gary Orona, of the Philippines, for your graphical talent and fast assistance.

The blessings in my life include all the good and talented people I have met. Incredibly, no challenge is too complex when folks work together on a common goal.

Cover from Pixabay. com

COPYRIGHT

Registered with ISBN or Writers Guild

9798695724776

9781672442275 Paperback

OTHER BOOKS BY G.H. WHITE

A Touch of Evil
The Life and Love of a Knuckleballer
Sgt. Ma Space Soldier
God's Gate
Heart-Shaped Memories
Her Passion to Kill
An Elite Killing Team (sequel, Her Passion to Kill) Stalking Evil (book 3 of Her Passion to Kill)
The Many Paths of Lenny

PROLOGUE

Sergeant Ma, Recruiter

Greetings.

I welcome all listening to this tachyonic broadcast from multiple planets and star systems.

Humanity spread includes hot, cold, dry, and wet planets, with gravitational fields plus or minus 1 G (or 1Gal Galileo). Some of your planets rotate around two suns. Others have three. Some of your worlds have nothing more advanced than bacteria, while others are teeming with different lives.

Perhaps you are trained to maintain your food sources via molecular disposition machines. Or, maybe you work on electrolysis oxygen creation machines.

Many of you find your purpose in medicine, mining, electronics, etc.

But, all your planets are subject to unwelcome intrusions from other places wanting to take what you work so hard to produce.

That is why the All Worlds United Armed Services exist; to keep our people as safe as possible.

I am a soldier, armed and ready to engage any aggressor from any planet or star system.

I was born and trained for warfare.

My expectations include bleeding wounds and late-night regrets of losing comrades-at-arms.

People speak of the end of the world and peace for all humankind. I think both concepts are dreamlike and elementary.

One is fatally pessimistic regarding a future doom as inevitable. The other is overly optimistic, as if humanity can learn to get along together, thereby ending warfare.

Human nature has not changed in the last ten thousand years and will not likely improve in the future. There have always been bullies, criminals, and murderers, and that will continue.

The New Universal All Worlds Wikipedia lists a soldier as typically an enlisted man.

I take exception to the NUAW Wikipedia in that; I am not a man and am similar to man.

I have genetically modified genes from Old Earth.

My enlistment is in the UAS Space Brigade. In common vernacular, I am a Space Soldier.

Major General Harris ordered me to describe my arc from my beginnings until now to encourage you to consider a future in the UAS.

If you are still listening to this recording, we need you badly.

Major Harris said I should include my successes and failures, so anyone viewing this broadcast would understand that a proper attitude is essential.

She felt it would help recruitment efforts for the UAS if I recounted my story, as it is unique enough to allow any of you on the fence to climb down and join me in the UAS.

The recruitment data indicates that many of you will not want to give up and leave your ancestral home, though worn out as it now is from wars and overpopulation.

Let me encourage you to see the Cosmos.

See with your fresh eyes, worlds both far and bright. Worlds so different from your own that you will marvel at them. You will smell the air that has not been contaminated by humanity. You will see diverse animals in person rather than on a vid monitor.

You will hear languages from people quite different from your own.

Yes, Universal English is spoken, but not by every person. Local dialects are frequently preferred.

Many of you will have adventures you cannot imagine at this point.

Sadly, a few of you will die in the UAS, but your family will be promptly rewarded for your service and loss.

My present assignment is on Crageor3, which orbits the star Wolf359. This star is 7.8 light-years from Old Earth.

You can call me Sgt. Ma. I am afraid you could not pronounce my given name. I have not met an Earthling/Terraen that could repeat the whistles and clicks we use on Aleutin.

I like to use the word Terraen from the old Latin phrase Terra Firma, or solid, for any planet.

Many civilizations in our galaxy are trying to thrive, mostly in trade with other worlds. Some planets might be rich in minerals, while others might not. Some might have an abundance of water, others not.

Still, some aggressors will steal or kill rather than put in the hard work others use to produce.

War goes on, and some profit handsomely from the wars. Some say that if two people are left standing, one will bully the other, and a small war will begin.

My homeworld, Aleutin, orbits the binary system of Sirus, such that I grew up with two suns and long hours of daylight, with shorter hours of dark. I will explain more about this later.

Many of you know the technical challenges we overcame in centuries past to move from one star to another.

The old nuclear reactors, chemical rockets, and solar sails of the 21st, 22nd, and partially into the 23rd century would only work at sub-light speeds. There were too many drawbacks and challenges for that period to travel faster than light.

Even the nearest star system Alpha Centauri at 4.37 light-years from Old Earth, would take over 5.5 years to reach it using those ancient rocket engines. One had to account for the spaceship to speed up near sub-light and decelerate to enter a star system; one constant speed was not possible.

Some seven hundred years ago, my ancestors descended from a human when only sub-light speed was available. Therefore, my foremothers made their initial trip in hibernation, spending ten years to arrive at Aleutin, a system 8.6 light-years from Old Earth.

Many think of Space as a pure vacuum, but early travelers found dust between the solar systems likely left after the Big Bang.

A 50microgram bit of sand is only an irritant in a planet's wind blowing at 100 kilometers an hour.

But, if I use this same bit of sand and speed it up near the speed of light, it will punch through a spaceship, likely destroying all inside. For your physics buffs, you will remember Force equals Mass times Acceleration or F = ma.

So, space dust is a real problem, as this specific failure occurred more often in the near-light starships of yesteryear than anyone wants to remember. There were frequent losses of life.

Though it is common knowledge that modern interstellar star drives have made traveling from one star to another possible, it took humankind a long time to invent the systems we enjoy today. The other species that beat us to the stars did not share their technology.

Therefore we had to create our own.

It would be timely if you remembered old Earth's sun is five billion years old from your science classes, while the Big Bang happened almost fourteen billion years ago. Old Earth and its sun were considered babies to systems closer to the middle of our galaxy, as some of those solar systems were several billion years older than ours. Therefore, Earth's technological progress was overshadowed by other older species closer to the center of the Milky Way Galaxy.

We learned that star-to-star travel is possible if one can fold the fabric of the space-time continuum, but it requires vast amounts of energy.

Imagine a piece of paper with the furthest points at each page's ends. Fold the article, and now the points almost touch each other. Hence, star to star requires warping and bending the space-time fabric.

Star drives are not safe within a star system, as they are sometimes guilty of causing time shifts in nearby worlds and lives. Reports of loss or gain of an hour happened, but there were also cases of days.

Losing or gaining time was very unsettling to the people living through the shift.

Space businesses found that getting one spaceship to do star and planet travel did not make economic sense.

Star-to-star travel does not require fancy seats, shower stalls, air cleaning, or food, but interplanetary does. It was much more efficient to concentrate on one design for each. After all, hibernation equipment is standard in an interplanetary ship but not needed from star to star.

Scientists dropped chemical rocketry in the 22nd century. Today we enjoy various space engines to do the job of traveling from planet to planet. These include solar sails moving on a photon stream from a nearby star, nuclear pulse engines, plasma, or wave-induced electromagnet engines.

Intra planetary travel is comparatively slow, so travelers frequently travel in hibernation rather than carrying vast supplies of food, oxygen, and water for the weeks and months necessary to complete the journey in some larger star systems.

For example, from your Old Earth to Mars was a journey of nine months out and back, circa 2075. The first few missions were one-way trips to Mars.

People were waking from hibernation to speak of their mouths' headaches, nausea, and strange tastes. These same never bothered me. Before joining the UAS, I mostly used interplanetary ships to travel, so I am more accustomed to hibernation techniques.

Since joining the UAS, I have traveled more star to star than in my past. If you enlist, you will as well.

For emphasis, Star travel requires enormous energy to create the gravitational and electromagnetic fields to achieve this folding of space-time fabric. These engines' fuel comes from a quickly decaying element called Ununpentium 115 with an atomic weight of 288. It is rare today and costly, but it is presently the only way to develop the power needed to fold space-time fabric.

Via the electromagnetic fields, engines focus on a swirling microscopic vortex in front of the ship, pulling huge graviton fields towards it until the fabric tears or opens.

One could visualize a wood screw starting a tiny hole in a bit of lumber, but as the screw turns, it forces itself deeper into the material, making a more massive hole.

This electromagnetic screw both opens the space-time fabric and pulls the craft forward into the fold. The gravitational fields remain huge until the ship can pass through.

Let's call this the entry hole. And, since we have folded the fabric, the exit hole is the entry mirror, but now an immense distance has been traveled.

To the star traveler, this happens in mere seconds.

The actual path to and through the portal, and the destination, are mapped with quantum computers. These control the gravitational engines in all dimensions since they use Quantum Entanglement, which is interdimensional.

Two centuries ago, in the early stages of development, one could find oneself inside a star or planet upon exiting the fabric. All present-day reports show that specific travel and a life-ending problem no longer happen.

During the historical events, loss of life was frequent, and the earliest pilots had tremendous courage even to try.

There are several critical differences between Old Earth and my homeworld, Aleutin. Earth orbits one star, for instance, while Aleutin orbits a binary of two stars, called the Sirus System.

One Sirus star is a white dwarf located 61.5 million solar kilometers from Aleutin. The other is a G-class star 8.2 million solar kilometers from home.

From Old Earth, one could see Sirus A without a telescope, not B. Strangely, a few Old Earth cultures knew of both A and B.

No one knows why this is so, though wild speculation exists even today.

One famous African culture, called the Dogon tribe, had wooden devices that accurately tracked Sirus A and B centuries before the telescope.

Without a telescope, how did the Dogon tribe know of Sirus B?

The combined amount of radiation reaching the surface of Aleutin is two times more robust than on Old Earth. On a given day, you might have about 1360 watts per square meter striking your planet's surface, while we have a heart-warming 2800 watts per square meter.

Without protection, the least you would get is skin cancer on Aleutin. We Aleutians are much darker than you, and our genes were modified to handle these extremes.

Our ocean tides are more severe depending on the planet's

rotation and position of the two suns than your sun and moon cause on Old Earth.

On the plus side, our oceans are healthier and cleaner than yours because of these tidal changes, boasting many sea lives.

Our winds are more severe as they frequently reach 100 kilometers per hour. Our foremothers' construction techniques have proven adequate to keep our buildings intact, but during our earlier years, there was a learning process and frequent loss of shelter.

I like the windy days. The air inside of a spaceship has too many uncomfortable smells for me.

The typical daytime temperatures on Aleutin are 40C-50C or so. I am sure this is too warm for you that have pure Old Earth genetics.

I do not mean any offense, just stating facts over feelings and letting you know there are many differences you can experience if you join the UAS visiting other worlds.

Though they were still playing with synthesizing ribonucleic acid, Old Earth's 22nd-century geneticists bred us for this radiation and heat.

However, with the advances of quantum computing, computer imaging, information sharing worldwide, and a significant advancement in ruby lasers, the geneticists made a considerable discovery late in that century.

The scientists finally understood the DNA wrapping order.

The scientists could then account for heart disease and blond hair, but manipulating code to make changes was dicey and prone to many scientific failures.

My foremothers, or our original gene suppliers, were one of the earlier experiments that had their DNA re-ordered via the recombinant method using CRISPER, and a few pieces of code changed.

One noticeable code change was the growth DNA, EcoR1, as we are all taller than most of you. There were others, as well, explaining our tolerance for heat, radiation, and so forth.

None of Aleutin die of skin cancer as a result.

Since nature doesn't like to be trifled with, she retaliated by changing the sex codes without the original geneticists' knowledge.

Yes, we are all female and self-replicating. That's right; we can have our children without outside interference.

Before we start with all the jokes, let me tell you, I have heard them all. I know about the Benusian Midget and the Aleutinite in the shower, and I know about the bald aerial cop from Old Earth with three Aleutinites in the hotel room. And I know the difference between a wet nurse and an Aleutinite.

So, just stow it! OK? I hope you are smiling at the humor. I am. I like the jokes.

On the positive side, however, we have little need for politicians or lawyers, as you people from Old Earth do.

Baby doctors are in short supply, however.

I can't speak for all the gals there on my homeworld, but I sort of wish that we had a few men. I mean, they would offer a viewpoint missing from Aleutin. Although I am sort of 'butch,' I sometimes appreciate a man’s point of view.

My time with the military has been excellent in that regard.

I have sent a copy of my enlistment into the UAS for your reading, demonstrating the attitude that Major General Harris wanted me to share with you. Which is one of perseverance and “can do.”

In summary, that is my background, and now you know I was born for the All Worlds United Armed Services, and I love being a soldier.

I heartily encourage all listening to consider enlisting in the

UAS to see the Cosmos.

ONE

Ma’s Enlistment

Before joining the UAS, I had been part of the Planet Militia for seven standard years.

This PM force kept the peace on Aleutin and the other four planets within the Sirus system. I was glad to be part of the PM.

But my sights had been on the Universal Armed Services since I first saw their aquamarine uniforms about ten standard years ago. I knew they would look good on me.

The UAS is co-ed, but they wouldn't let me enlist at first because they didn't think I could handle the environment. Their confusion depends on one's point of view that I am attracted to my sex because that is all I know. Or, I will go gaga upon seeing the men for the first time.

Neither is true.

When you have your sex partner and race creator as a built-in appliance, not an add-on, looking for an external sex partner is not lust nor race-driven.

We Aleutians do not find your pale skin and eyes attractive. I would assume that you would find me equally unattractive.

And your people are so short that I have yet to meet an Old Earth Terraens taller than my shoulders. I hear that New Earth has some taller specimens with less than 1 Gal gravity.

Since I was a child, I have wanted to be in the military.

Mom, my gene Supplier, decided that I was Planet Militia material because I was overly aggressive as a child. I received my share of bruises but gave more than I got. Other moms complained too much about how I treated their children. Some were larger than I, but none were as aggressive.

Mom pushed me to military schools to channel that aggression. That is where I found my calling. They taught me all the proper ways for saluting, dressing, firing an Argonia rifle, and so on, in the Militia.

I excelled in hand-to-hand techniques. I majored in military tactics. I learned various ways of dealing with situations that involved taking lives or destroying enemy resources.

A saboteur, you might say. I thrived in this environment.

One day, my rebellious nature was tested when I wanted to progress and enter the UAS while leaving Planet Militia.

During a leave, I hopped a Neubian freighter bound for the nearest recruitment station on Middletary. Since it was only three weeks of travel by nuclear pulse engines, I did not use hibernation.

The Middletary recruiters told me I could not enlist because I did not fit the profile.

Wait!

I had traveled in the cargo hold of a noisy, stinky Neubian freighter to Middletary to enlist, and they would not let me into the UAS?

Oh, my intelligence was high enough, and I passed my physical exam with flying colors. But the enlistment officers started by telling me I was oversized by thirty percent.

No girl likes to hear that. As Aleutinites go, I am petite. I may not be a gene supplier model, but I believe that I am attractive.

Lieutenant Huxley's recruiter said, “I am sorry, but UAS Starion Class Plasma ships are not equipped for your sexual orientations.”

I said, “I am a woman, just like your women. I can use the same facilities!"

Lt. Huxley said, "You are not like our women. Our women can't have children without help or sit inside an oven like a sauna. Nor pick up a Buick! You do not fit the profile!"

What is a Buick?

Anyway, my rebellious nature surfaced. I mean, they hurt my feelings, you know?

As my anger simmered, I developed a plan.

Rather than hopping the next freighter back to my homeworld, I reconnoitered the area and found a base camp for myself. On a rock-strewn hillside, I found a cave big enough to accommodate me and deep enough so I could hide from someone walking past.

Since the entire camp seemed so relaxed, procuring food, tools, and such was easy for someone trained as I was. Most of what I needed seemed to be lying around, waiting for me to pick it up.

I found one Argonia plasma rifle lying outside a portapotty.

Argonia rifles make a nasty horizontal slice in whatever they hit. The cut is only four molecules wide but will penetrate any substance short of diamonds.

One can be quite the artist with one of these. I made five well-placed shots from a snipers' position, some ten klicks away from the base. This action caused the UAS certification personnel to scramble as their building leaned more towards the sun than before my shot.

I cut only three of the support pedestals. I could have taken them all out.

I think it improved the building's architecture and lines.

Next, I placed two perfect shots into the laser navigation system for good measure. Since they had no laser nav, there would not be incoming fresh supplies for the troops.

I fumed all night long, still angry at the UAS rejection.

I hit them again before dawn.

As the dwarf sun colored the horizon in greenish hues, I had already reversed the phasing on the sonoplexors, thereby destroying their charging capacitors.

With the sonoplexors inoperative, Middletary's insects were free to come near and into the troop facilities.

Middletary is a relatively new planet for humans, so there had been little time to adapt to living successfully there.

The first colonists had enormous difficulties with the insects. The ones that crawled ate or ruined most of the food stores. The ones that flew bit viciously, resulting in a loss of limbs and sometimes, death.

A few of the insects were more prominent than a Terraens' hand.

The sonoplexors helped keep the insects at bay with a high-frequency warbling sound.

I could see the certification personnel got the sonoplexors back online to repel the dreaded insects near noon through my field glasses.

Sick Call that afternoon filled to the brim.

One young man had a particularly nasty bite. It seems he was relieving himself behind the Protonous stockpile when he was bit.

I wonder if he kept his tiny appendage, or did it fall to the ground?

That afternoon, I decided that their electrical generators needed tuning. These engines rotated at a pleasant 1800 Revolutions Per Minute, producing perfect electrical voltage for all the power supplies on base. By revolving the stator wheel another ten degrees, I moved them to 2400 RPM.

Thus, overvoltage destroyed many computers and other electrical devices before they were sharp enough to shut down their power source.

Boy, they were mad!

Tuesday night, and I was bored. I decided to hit their environmental chambers.

Most humans get uncomfortable when the humidity hits 95 percent and the temperature gets very far from 22C degrees. So, the personnel was notably disturbed when the air temperature hit 0 C degrees, and the moisture moved to 100 percent.

Ice formed on all surfaces, and the air glittered with frozen moisture falling slowly into the rooms.

I heard some new Old English words. It was highly descriptive and colorful.

I guess the sudden ice in the hallways was treacherous and rather bothersome to the barefooted ones.

The following greenish dawn broke, and I was hot-footing it back to my hidden quarters, but I paused with a thought.

Their perimeter security system had an obvious flaw in it. It would be simple to tune in to the security sensor frequencies, describe the code, and change it for my use.

I targeted their 'planet invasion' alarm. It sounded like the horn rotated 360 degrees every 15 seconds for fifteen minutes.

There were very few good ears left in the certification camp to perform or refuse enlistment because the alarm was one hundred and twenty decibels.

I moved into their encampment at noon through another breach I created in their perimeter system. The food stores had had some damage from the day before.

By changing the Protonous heat levels, lowering the valence band energy levels, and adding a little diesel oil to the stock, I changed their eating habits for the next two weeks while awaiting fresh supplies.

Of course, they had to repair the nav system first, so there were no new supplies.

Well—you get the picture.

That night, I set up an optically coupled resonance projector. A few personnel were stirring about inside their quarters one hour past green dawn.

One soldier, holding his second cup of coffee, looked outside, past a Paledian Palm, and saw a herd of Bisudian Dragons. He dropped his cup onto his lap.

Bisudian Dragons stand fifteen feet tall and are particularly mean. With quick rear legs, they can run down most prey. They have relatively large mouths, one meter across. Their teeth are only fourteen centimeters long, however. They hold their game in their mouths with these teeth and then use their 110 centimeters long tongues to ram holes in their victim. Then they alternately squeeze their victims and drink the blood.

These Dragons can cover half a mile in their dining. Because of their range habits, the Dragons can return to the kill zone and kill again.

Naturally, this disturbed the Recruitment Personnel's breakfasts. They fired through their open portals at this herd, again and again. Frustration levels were very high, and many openly wept since the Dragons did not run away or die.

It took a long time for a single member (healthy soldier) to run a computer check and determine that there were no Bisudian Dragons or Paledian Palms outside.

They were only moving holographs created by my projector.

One hour later, I came into their encampment again.

Again, I asked to enlist.

"Huh? What did you say?" the young female soldier, Specialist four Thoren, asked at the top of her lungs.

I noted she had hands behind each ear. "Speak up! The planet invasion alarm whacked my hearing."

I increased my volume and asked again to enlist.

Again, she refused. She emphatically shook her head.

This time, I asked for the C.O. As their Commanding Officer had been affected by an insect bite and was indisposed, she also denied this request.

I then asked for the standing C.O. that was his temporary replacement.

With a heavy sigh, Specialist four Thoren said, "Ok. But it will not help you. I will summon Ensign Clinton.

When visibly shaken, Clinton arrived, he said, "I can give you five minutes. So, make your case."

I showed Ensign Clinton my training disk, with all its associated history of my Planet Militia experiences and advances.

He was slightly interested, but his fever kept him from total concentration.

"How did you get contract fever, Sir?" I asked so innocently.

Ensign Clinton responded with, "An insect bite. The insects here are vicious. And, Saboteurs are attacking our base. They are systematically ruining our encampment and the health of all base personnel."

He looked at me, shook his head, and said, "We can't carry on much longer, and if the C.O. does not recuperate or they do not stop their attack, it will force us to evac or die."

"Sir, if you will view subsection 4.1.7. of my training disc, you will notice that I have certification as an educator in the act of sabotage and counter-sabotage!" I said.

He now looked at me with a side-long glance filled with suspicion. Now, I had his entire interest.

I said with a smile, "If I were an enlisted member, I could bring this knowledge to bear and save your personnel from further discomfort."

The dawn of realization slowly crawled upon his brow as his

eyes widened.

"Whem, 4.1.7., you say?" Ensign Clinton asked. "How long have you been trying to enlist?" the good Ensign asked politely.

I hung my head and shook it at the ground, “Mournfully, I must admit to several days of enlistment attempts.”

I snapped my head up and put my hands out in a defensive posture.

"Nothing against your personnel. Everyone was just doing their respective jobs. I am sure there was nothing personal in how they performed those jobs while rejecting my enlistment."

I noticed that his left leg was twitching, and the hand on that side was also. Another insect might have just bitten him.

"Based on what you know now, can you guarantee that you can make the sabotage cease?" The good Ensign asked.

I proudly said, "I am prepared to guarantee that nothing will happen from the time I enlist! I will use counter-espionage techniques and stop the saboteur."

Ensign Clinton swung around and ran up to the female soldier that had previously denied my request.

"Spec four Thoren, get her all necessary paperwork to sign and do it A.S.A.P. I want her measured, suited, and billeted before nightfall! I want to see her Basic Training schedule on my desk in forty-five minutes. I want her shipped out of here on the very first transport we can find. Now! I mean now!" the Ensign said while Spec Thoren had one hand behind each ear.

She caught enough of his words to think of a sarcastic response, but she held it.

He started to walk away, but the twitching made him stop. He turned, looked directly into my eyes, and said,

"I will make sure she gets treated with respect. Her training has earned her more than the typical recruit. I will make her a First Sergeant to ensure that we will not have any more saboteurs in our midst. I will make it a field promotion based on her vast previous experience and training record!”

"But, Ensign Sir, regulations prohibit such a field promotion. She is not even Regular Army. She is just Planet Militia!" Thoren said.

I was getting irritated again. I looked around at the base, and my eyes quickly ran to the portapotty facilities erected on the planet's surface. They were a cream color, with one door for each facility.

In true military fashion, all lay in a perfect line. I figured that one concussion grenade at just the right location would do the trick!

This action would create one hell of a mess if you could excuse my pun.

Ensign Clinton had watched my eyes and saw where they had settled.

"Spec. Thoren, I am the Standing C.O. You know that field battle promotions are part of my responsibility for acts of war or siege. We are in an active siege. I have given you a direct order! Make it so!"

At that moment, Ensign Clinton's nose was a military centimeter from Spec Thoren's nose while his hand and leg twitched again.

"You will follow my field directive. You will treat this as a direct order. Or I will put you on duty—Tonight! You will be Policing the OUTBACK of Nigella four! I will send you there on an escape pod. Maybe you will make it, and maybe you won’t. But, either way, you will make enlistee Ma, Sergeant Ma."

Specialist Thoren followed orders as she had heard of the challenge of Nigella four. The reports included a microscopic species that crawled on the ground en masse in the hundreds of millions. These critters would surround their prey, relentlessly taking the tiniest of bites until the victim ceased to exist.

Spec Thoren immediately gathered the documents necessary for a field promotion. She fed them to me to sign as quickly as she could.

It was happening! I would become UAS. And a First Sergeant.

I felt so proud of my recent achievements. I could live my dream and show my gene supplier that I was more than just overly aggressive.

I would even have official papers and a new Sergeant badge to prove it to her the next time I saw her.

I sat down on a nearby rock with all papers signed to gloat. This day was wonderful, and I wanted to savor it.

Later, I would learn that I had gained respect unwittingly as my enlistment story spread throughout the UAS. The legend of me grew as distance and time went on.

From my enlistment forward, wherever I went, the soldiers were honorable to me, gave me the best bunk, and usually kept a respectable distance away from me.

In my presence, there were no Aleutinian jokes.

After enlistment, I had two planet falls, in different solar systems, to work under challenging circumstances. I cannot give you the details, as they are Military Secrets.

But I was assigned to find the bad guys and protect the good ones. Dispatching the bad guys took a lot of Argnoia's power.

I was lucky that the soldiers around me provided all the support anyone could need.

I had excellent superiors in each case that wanted me to succeed.

So, when a ground pounder says, "It’s the system, and you can't change it!" Just think of me.

I love the UAS.

TWO

A New Sergeant and Friend

The UAS assigned Sergeant Ma to Rigel 2 for her first UAS duty assignment.

The troop carrier UASS Brigette Nelson that ferried her to this system was much older than any she had been on before. It smelled of the many souls on her deck from decades past.

Grime was seemingly everywhere, while the deck androids swabbed, scrubbed, and repainted where necessary.

Sgt. Ma guessed the grime source was caused by a century or more of recycled air and countless bodies.

CO2 and particulate filters could remove so much concentrated human presence, including sweat, smells, dander, and dirt.

Since this was only a two-week journey, most of the onboard troops did not go into hibernation. Many felt it would be a waste to sleep when the soldiers preferred to eat, talk, read, listen to music, and enjoy this short holiday from their regular duties.

She found her fellow navy and ground pounders got along very well, though the sound level would approach zero when they saw her in a passage or common area.

Ma knew her physical presence daunted some of them, as most were less than two meters tall, while she was two and a half.

She knew this would end when the personnel achieved planetfall. Squads generally bonded quickly in combat, and she knew she would then fit in.

Though her military quarters were cramped, she had more room than the common soldier received. In hers, they had removed the other bunks, leaving just one.

She placed a small nightstand at the very end of her bunk to allow her feet to drape over. She then put a simple pillow on the nightstand for her feet. The small changes extended her bunk enough to accommodate her height, though turning over in her sleep was a problem.

Luckily, she only needed 3-4 hours a night.

The bathroom facilities were a bit cramped, but she made them work. She would not complain.

Sgt. Ma made conversational friends with Captain Redding, who likely followed the human belief to keep friends close and enemies closer.

Captain Redding had little experience with Aleutins, and thus, Sgt. Ma was an unknown to her, an alien.

Since they got along well and spent a lot of time together, Captain Redding said, “Ma, if it is just the two of us alone, call me Alice.”

Alice seemed interested in her background as a female ground pounder and saboteur.

“You are the first Aleutinite I have met in the UAS. Most prefer to stay near your homeworld!” Captain Redding said.

Sgt. Ma considered this and said, “I am not sure I am the first, but probably one of few. You are correct, though. My sisters do tend to stay on our planet. When you are used to the heat of Aleutin and move into spaceships, it is colder than most would like. I adapted because I wanted to.”

It was evident to Capt. Redding this last, Ma said with a touch of pride.

Ma discovered that Captain Alice Redding was also interested in hand-to-hand martial arts, and she found that Alice was quick and well-versed.

She and Ma would feign fighting to keep their skills up while still practicing their kata or organized sequence moves.

Eventually, the two became familiar with each other's methods of performing moves and countermoves.

No one could ignore Sgt. Ma's imposing presence, but Alice was looking for ways to make it less of a problem.

Both Judo and Jiu-Jitsu would offer leverage for a taller and stronger component. She thought leg strikes to knock Ma off balance was her best way. If she could get Ma on the ground, she reasoned, using various arm or leg locks to neutralize her.

The problem was that Ma was very catlike, and though Alice sometimes would remove one foot and leg from the ground, Ma would seem to regain balance quickly.

Captain Redding learned her speed was her greatest weapon against Ma, as even though Ma was quick on her own, her larger limbs required more time to bring into action.

But, aside from combat training, Ma listened eagerly to Captain Redding's stories involving men and how they reacted to a military woman since she had so little experience on her own.

For Redding's part, she was envious that Ma did not have to seek men out to procreate.

As Captain Redding replied when Ma asked her about marriage, "Well, to tell you the truth, that is the only reason I would marry some guy. To have children, you know? No doubt, I could go into a lab, pick a donor, and have the child. But, aside from descriptions and pictures stuck on his record, I would know very little about him. I would see the child grow and wonder if I saw my traits or the invisible donor. And, of course, I could adopt one. But my instincts are to have one more naturally. I want to see the father, hear him, touch him, and then meet the child. I know that sounds so old-fashioned. In a lab, I could pay the gene splicers to dial in the baby's genes to make them stronger, smarter, and to look like me or anyone else. In my mind, we would marry, have the child, then divorce, but he would still be around to help me raise the child. Maybe that is just a dream, but it is my dream."

Redding also said, "But the military is enough for now. It is truly all I ever wanted."

Sgt. Ma asked her, "Captain, do you dislike men that much?"

Redding laughed a little and said, "I just find so many of them have huge egos, wanting to order a woman. Some of their emotional responses remind me of our past cave dwellers. Yes, I guess I do dislike most of them. But I can stand them as long as they follow my orders."

Ma could easily follow this logic, so she nodded her head in understanding.

Aside from men, she and Alice covered many other topics. Ma did not use any makeup and was unsure why Earth women did.

Alice explained, "Earth women always want to look their best. Ancient Egypt Old Earth Queen Cleopatra used various ingredients to make her lips look fuller and redder. It must have been quite hard to do in her day, but she made it work. Some of those ingredients were disgusting, so she wanted it badly. It just became part of the culture, just like we love shopping, while the men do not normally care for shopping or makeup."

Sgt. Ma was confused again, "What is shopping? Oh, you mean buying something you need from someone else? We don't have shopping on Aleutin."

Captain Alice Redding giggled a little and said, "Well, you can toss out the word need. Our shopping is more like what we want, though we cover our purchases with the word need. For instance, most of us have far more shoes than we will ever wear. Color or style for every occasion."

Ma just stared at her. Why would someone own more than they need? What purpose would that serve? Wouldn't that just be wasteful?

Captain Redding rounded out Ma's insufficient knowledge of Rigel 2 and how violent it had become in the last few weeks.

There were two sides to civil conflict on the planet. Thousands had died in pitched battles, leaving no one side in charge.

In simplistic terms, one side wanted to strip mine large areas of the planet as both lithium and silver were in ample supply.

The other side wanted the countryside left alone for crop growth. Both sides felt they were serving the needs of humankind.

At the very least, the growers demanded traditional deep mining techniques to leave most of the planet undisturbed. Strip mining was much less expensive and quicker, but it ruined an asteroid or planet's surface.

What started as an environmental dispute boiled over when someone executed the miners' Chief, live for the news vid.

During that time frame, Chief Tuttle was the growers' elected leader, and he was their most crucial voice until they transmitted his dead image.

His suspended body showed various cuts to his torso, while his blood ran down to his bare feet suspended above the floor.

While he cried for his life, his executioners used an enormous blade to slice open his belly horizontally, allowing his intestines to spill out.

Pandemonium took place. People died that day within hours of the broadcast.

Though firearms were forbidden planet-wide, weapons were brutal as any heavy object or kitchen knife would be wielded to pound, shred, or stab whoever was at hand.

To someone standing neutral, it would have been difficult to tell who was killing who.

The UAS had landed a small party two weeks ago to begin to slow the massacres.

Ma was part of a larger group to stop the carnage. A negotiated peace treaty would be the outcome.

After Captain Redding's summary, Sgt. Ma thought she saw a place for herself, relying on her past abilities.

"Captain Redding, I believe I might be useful to find out the most dangerous ones behind the violence rather than fighting on the skirmish lines. If you remove the bullies, calmer minds can talk and find a resolution." Ma said.

Redding looked at her, imagining the Aleutian woman trying to blend in with the crowd on Rigel 2.

Sneaking around did not seem to work in her mind. Since most of the group was from Old Earth, she believed Ma would stick out easily.

Captain Redding avoided her base thoughts and asked, "How could you achieve that?"

Sgt. Ma said, "Well, it is part of my nature and training. I realize you imagined what I looked like and could not picture me being successful. But I have various ways of pulling a rabbit out of a hat." Sgt. Ma was so pleased that she had finally understood an Earth phrase and how to use it.

THREE

Rigel 2, Subdue the Violence

The troopship made orbit around Rigel 2, and a planet lander docked with it.

The soldiers began their transfer to the planet lander. The soldiers would only get weapons and munitions on the planet's surface.

Within a few hours, Sgt. Ma found herself at the temporary UAS station on Rigel 2 in the city of Delaware.

She was not surprised to see Captain Redding assigned her to her unit and four full squads. Each squad had 8-10 soldiers, but these were all highly trained personnel.

Underneath the military tent composed of a thin white material that moved in the wind like a breathing creature, Captain Redding gave them all a briefing on the local population.

She included how one might identify one side from the other. The clothing was an essential thing they could use, as one side tended towards silks and were clean-shaven, while the other preferred denim and wore beards and cloth wrappings on their heads.

"Remember, you are here as military police. You will not interfere with the normal functioning of this world. We will encourage peace. If violence takes place, the UAS will take over. Then, you are authorized to use deadly force at my command. You can only use deadly force without me if your life is in danger.

It must be your last resort. Do I make myself clear?" Captain Redding said to all.

The group of soldiers responded, "Yes, sir, Captain!"

She then assigned each squad to specific duty stations around the city, pointing at a map to show them where.

Other officers were doing similar tasks in different places on the planet.

Captain Redding then said, "Weapons in a ready firing position, but on safe. All of you, move out!"

She placed a light hand on Sgt. Ma's sleeve keeps her from moving with the others.

"Ok, Sgt. It might be best if I do not tell you what to do using your training. I do not need details until you are successful. That will give me plausible denial ability. Try not to kill unless you have no choice. Try not to be killed. Does that sound reasonable to you?" Redding finished.

Ma smiled slightly and responded with a sharp salute and click of her boot heels.

"Yes, Captain. I will do my very best."

Captain Redding continued, "Use your communicator and send me encrypted messages about your progress. Use the IL22 encryption key. Hardly anyone uses that one."

"Yes, Captain," Ma nodded, grabbed her device, and keyed in the encryption code.

Only the Captain and she would be using that one.

Even if someone could intercept her frequency and record the transmission, it would be almost impossible to pick the correct encryption, thereby understanding the message.

Sgt. Ma already knew where she wanted to get started.

Ma began to type into her palm computer, looking for the electronic databases for the local news channels' reruns.

Chief Tuttle's execution was the one she needed.

She watched the same segment repeatedly. She saw the face of the executioner utilizing a large knife to disembowel the growers' leader.

But that was not what she wanted from the recorded piece. After several viewings, she was sure the killer looked at someone off-camera for the go-ahead to kill the helpless suspended man.

Now, she changed her perspective of the viewing, as she did not need to watch the killing again but looked at other objects in the recording for additional clues.

There was none except the killer's eyes moving to someone off-camera, followed by a slight nod and grim smile.

Now she had to move on to her following electronic research, as she needed to find the killer in other recordings, using her special facial recognition software to see who stood near him.

That would be her target, more so than the killer just following orders.

She wanted the silent boss.

In prior news recordings of angry mobs, she caught sight of the killer several times.

In a few, a rather large balding and bearded man was in his perimeter. She focused on him and noticed he used his waist-level hands to give orders to the surrounding ones.

He never spoke in any of these mob events, but the killer did.

The killer was the mouthpiece, the focus, to allow the man behind the scene anonymity.

She just needed one clear view of his face, and she would have her target.

A few hours later, she finally found one recording of the man with a full beard and balding head standing a few feet away from the killer.

Her military-grade facial recognition software would tie into the electronic databases on this planet via her military computers on other worlds.

She executed the go command and sat back to allow herself to relax.

While she waited, she thought back to an earlier plan to get close to this mob. But suddenly, she had a new idea.

She only needed the one, the boss, and not the mob.

She thought that the facial recognition software was running much longer than expected, so this guy must have gone underground a long time ago.

A screen popped up, and she quickly read the list,

She read the screen to herself, "Aaron Kahn, last known residence Crageor 3, Silver Quarter. No known aliases. Priors include embezzlement, attempted rape, and 2nd-degree manslaughter, but nothing newer than 15 years ago.

Sgt. Ma thought to herself, "Whem. So you learned? You are smarter than the average crook. You learned how to make someone do your dirty work. You moved here for the silver profits, no doubt. Well, mister Aaron Kahn, your ass will belong to me soon."

Sgt. Ma smiled to herself and said, "I said ass. I used another Old Earth phrase."

Then, she activated the city's cameras with her military-grade facial recognition and told it, "find this rat!"

She ran the "executioner" in another window, though he was not as important. He quickly came back as Jad Baccus.

Interestingly, he had no criminal history but was wanted for desertion from Planet Militia on Crageor3. That is likely where the men met.

She knew from prior struggles that this part of the search would take hours, so she lay down on a nearby bench for some rest.

She must have fallen asleep as she heard a ding from the software and opened her eyes to see some small rodent perched on her chest. It had a voluminous tail, a slim brown furry body, and big black eyes. It was just staring at her. Maybe it knew she did not belong, or perhaps it was curious.

She blew air into its face, expecting it to jump and run. It did not. She slowly put one hand under its chest and lifted it from her own.

She put it carefully on the ground and went over to her electronics. The creature just stared at her from the same point she set it on the ground.

The software had found Aaron Kahn on several cameras, invariably leading up to a mob scene.

In most of the recordings, Aaron Kahn seemed to arrive on the stage from an area that looked like a mass transit system. When she accessed those cameras, she saw him exiting one train's cab like dozens of others. She tried running several backward to see if he came from a central point.

Ok. So, Kahn did not live local to Delaware; his residence was outside the city.

She set the alarm on each camera in each mass transit cab. A camera would show Kahn entering a cab, and then she would know which city he boarded the train.

She had to discover where he came from, where he lived. She could not rely on luck that he would come into her waiting arms.

Sgt. Ma suddenly had a suspicion, and as she glanced behind her, the creature was still staring at her.

Was it a spy device? Perhaps there was a camera hidden on its body. Maybe it was controlled by someone else.

She remembered that when she picked the creature up, its body temperature was low and she had neither felt a heartbeat nor breath moving into or out of its body. But, this might be normal here in this world.

Sgt. Ma thought, "That just might be a furry bug."

Ma had a triaxial device to locate invisible radio frequency signals. It was small enough to go into a jacket pocket. She found it with her back to the creature, turned it on to record, and slipped it inside her jacket.

Sgt. Ma turned back to the creature, bent over, and rubbed her extended fingers together to encourage it to come to her. The beast never moved.

She strode towards it. Just as she was about to touch it, it suddenly bolted and ran across the open ground until it reached a fence, which it jumped over.

She pulled the radio detection device from her pocket and ran it back a few minutes.

There was a low-level signal from when she hit record, but a continuous one.

Just as she was closing on the creature, the device recorded a sharp spike and another sharp point a few seconds later.

Now she knew the frequency of both the radio and the command lines.

Sgt. Ma assumed the first radio signal would have been when she turned to the creature, like an alert signal. And the second signal was telling the animal to turn and run.

The creature was out of her sight now.

Ma sent an encrypted electronic message to Captain Redding with a picture of the creature as a warning.

Sgt. Ma informed Captain Redding, "They know we are here. They are using small creatures as camera drones. This one looked somewhat like a squirrel. But now, we need to suspect birds or rodents. I have recorded its background radiofrequency and caught two spiked frequencies for commands. I suggest we inform all military what I have recorded and monitor these frequencies for an interception. Otherwise, our foe will know about our activities likely before we execute. My suspicion is, that they recorded your briefing today to the squads. I suggest you change your duty stations and commands to the troops you sent today. I would further advise that we encrypt all transmissions. Ma out!"

She was still irritated about what had happened but was grateful she had caught on as early as she had. The enemy knew what she looked like, as the little furry one probably did a complete body scan on her.

Even though sneaking around was not a good option before, it was impossible now. While she was thinking of it, Ma did a body scan of herself to ensure someone had not placed spy bugs on her person. Her detection equipment found nothing.

She knew that everything she had learned about Kahn and Baccus was suspect.

The table she used for her electronics was the kind humans would typically stand at, and the creature was ground level. It had a great view of her but a poor one of her electronics. How much could the animal's camera record from its vantage point on the ground?

Regardless, she had to assume that it had compromised the info.

She knew it blew this location, so she gathered her gear to find another.

She found a warehouse filled with plastic debris within half an hour, neatly bundled into large cubes. She surmised the plastic waste would be crushed and formed into these cubes.

The space looked empty and unused for weeks or months.

The dust on the floor seemed to be undisturbed, so that was an excellent sign to Ma.

Ma moved inside, keeping to the cubes' tops, and walked to the warehouse's far end.

There was a set of metal stairs leading upwards. At the top of the steps, she found one room above the warehouse to set up her gear. Usually, she would have put her warning sensors on the floor set for 25kilograms and up. But now, she knew it would have to warn her of any small creatures. She estimated the squirrel's weight near 2 kilograms. She moved the sensors to their lowest setting, hoping they would trigger.

She placed her cameras to monitor outside and inside the warehouse. Sgt. Ma set all cameras to alarm if either the "boss" or the executioner came within range.

She had plenty of MREs or meals ready to eat and water. Sgt. Ma decided now was a good time to eat an MRE and read a book.

She preferred psychology and philosophy, but today she read a romance novel, as Captain Redding's discussion on men made her very curious. She settled in for the long wait.

Three days passed, and Ma was still at her station, waiting. She had sent several encrypted messages to Captain Redding of her plans and status.

Redding replied to each with, "Understood. Over."

Via the internet, Ma knew the town was quiet. There were zero political outbreaks.

The military's presence invasion from the UAS appeared everyone was on their best behavior.

She had just torn her eyes from the cameras and data to return to another electronic book. She had finished the romance novel with more questions in her mind than answers. These questions had to wait until Captain Alice Redding had a relaxed time for discussions.

What do Earthling women and men act like when they are mating?

The book's intro used the word "steamy." Ma thought she understood the context now but needed certainty.

It was time to understand more about men, so she began a western novel about cowboys.

She had only read two pages when one mass transit alarm went off.

FOUR

The Mob

It was Kahn, and his executioner Baccus was with him.

The mass transit cab they had boarded was 11301, coming in from the southwest.

It was easy to pull up the route that 11301 ran each day, and from the timing of the signal, she knew where it had stopped.

This cab stopped in Thinning, 12 kilometers away from the city. The local internet provided details.

Thinning had a local population of 4,000. Most were miners. A combination of solar panels and windmills produced electricity.

The town was too small for things like schools or grocery stores. It had a mill store, so the miners would rack up credit there to be taken directly out of their pay. In most mining towns, the mills owned housing as well.

The person doing the physical mining labor got a small portion of the pay. Most went back to the mine owners in purchases from the store or rent of one house.

Via cameras, she watched the camera alarms go off as Kahn and Baccus moved through Delaware, triggering the ones along their path.

As they walked, more men would fall in behind them. What started as a line of 2 or 3 men were now a few dozen. She did not see any weapons, but she could tell several had hand-held signs as the column grew.

Ma triggered an encrypted message to Redding. She typed, "The boss and the executioner have arrived. Men are joining his column as he walks through the city. I think he is headed for the market center. May I suggest you gather your squads nearby but keep them out of sight to see what Kahn does? The last few men joining the mob appear to have printed signs, so maybe this is just for the local news channels."

She waited, and Redding replied, "Good Plan. Out."

Ma knew she could not go to the center herself. She stood above the crowd, so she stayed where she was. She turned on a local news channel to see how it played.

Ma believed that Kahn wanted the military to charge in to trigger a response and scream the UAS was interfering.

Still, the only thing that took place was Kahn's mob roving around the market square, brandishing their signs for the news cameras, screaming their slogans, "Miners have rights, Miners are important."

The news cameras showed none of the UAS aquamarine uniforms. Captain Redding never pulled the signal to charge and engage.

Kahn likely knew he only had fifteen minutes of local camera time, so from his vantage point, he caught the eye of Baccus and executed a chopping motion with one hand.

Baccus took a sign away from one in the mob and used it to hit an innocent bystander on the head. He was trying to generate violence.

But, the crowd gave way instead. These locals did not want to be mauled or sliced by the miners.

After a few minutes of nothing but mob activity, Kahn gave another hand signal, signaling back the way they had come in, and Baccus started to lead the mob out of the market center.

Sgt. Ma saw men peeling off from mob central in the cameras as it moved closer to the mass transit system.

Only half a dozen men were now left, walking with Baccus and Kahn.

The camera was best suited to show the men were poorly positioned to record the cab number. She could not tell which one they boarded. It left her to assume a return to Thinning.

She sent a message to Redding, "The targets have left the city. I believe I know where they are going. I may be out of communication range for a few days."

Sgt. Ma carefully packed her backpack.

She would have to travel quickly, so she removed unnecessary things.

Her electronics were crucial to come along, and most were light, small, and easy to pack.

Though there were various ways she could have gotten to Thinning, she had to stay off mass transit.

The distance was short enough that she could walk-run to the destination in a relatively short time frame. Once there, she would reconnoiter a safe place to set up shop, to wait for her opportunity.

The most direct route was a straight line; from her previous work, she knew there would be very little water along her way. She ensured both canteens were full and left the city to engage the countryside.

She marveled at the expansive view of the horizon, as there were no brush or trees above 2 meters high and no hills to notice.

The soil was reddish, primarily sand with rocky cover.

She might not have much to hide behind once she found Thinning.

Within 2 hours, she had made a visual sighting of Thinning.

Her compass and sense of distance had put her in proximity, but now, 0.5 kilometers from it, she knew she had to get low.

So, she low crawled from scrub to scrub, getting closer to the city.

The sun was now touching the land and would soon disappear below the horizon.

Darkness would be her time as she knew her Terraen counterparts could not see very far in the dark while she could.

"Thank you, gene splicers," she said to herself.

She used the remaining light to use her scope on her plasma rifle to look around town. She reasoned that since Kahn was such a hotshot in this world, he would likely have the most extensive house in the city.

The house would have armed and electronic security. As she scanned, she located two places that might be good ones. Strangely enough, they were very close together. The other townhouses were smaller and much more fundamental than those two, with environmentally ruined exteriors.

She found a nice rock and scrub bush to hide behind and settled in to let the night take over. She tried her communicator and found she had a small signal. She could not take the chance that someone in Thinning might have radio detection equipment, so she powered the communicator off.

FIVE

Infiltration

Sgt. Ma waited for the darkness to wrap the area in shadows of gray and black.

Ma left her pack behind the rock but took her plasma rifle and electronic sniffer.

The electronic sniffer had multiple functions and performed radio, magnetic, and audio detections and recordings.

She needed a warning for any cameras or motion detector devices in town.

She began her approach well after dark, betting she could get much closer than she presently was.

So she could glance at the meter while she kept her eyes downrange, she strapped the instrument to her plasma rifle.

The meter functions stayed near zero as she passed the few outer houses. It made a slight deviation for one house that had some electronic gaming taking place inside.

She glanced inside through a window. She saw one male in his underwear, wholly intent upon his game. She believed she would have to break the door down to get his attention.

Earlier, she had identified a broad dirt road that seemed to lead to the two larger and nicer houses. She stayed off it, walking down the shrub line, closer to the homes she passed so she could dive for cover if someone were out in the night.

The radio detection device stayed quiet, and she saw no personnel activity in the dark. She could not afford to let her guard down, so she stayed on point and alert the entire way.

Sgt. Ma needed half an hour to make it to the "nice" houses, but she went undiscovered.

This location is where she expected the detection device to start registering, but it stayed pretty still.

She was most worried about infrared, as the electronics needed for this technology did not use a lot of electrical current and might not register on her device.

She found a location between the two houses and hunkered down as it was comfortable to watch any activity.

Ma used the audio portion of her detector that would pipe amplified sound directly into her embedded earphones. She turned it on and pointed the audio receiver straight at one house, concentrating on windows, as sound would most easily transverse those.

She moved the instrument through each window. Zero.

She aimed the detector and plasma rifle at the second house and immediately picked up a low-volume conversation. She tried another window, and it was louder. She moved the audio receiver to the next window and lost the conversation. Back to the middle window she went.

She hit the record button and adjusted the gain to amplify the weak signal.

She had a hit. Four voices; one was called Aaron.

"Look, Aaron, I know you want to draw them out, but clubbing a guy in broad daylight could have just landed me in jail. It would not take them long to trace me back. I did it, but later I realized how stupid it was."

This speaker must be Jad Baccus, the executioner. Two other voices seemed to be agreeing with him.

Kahn spoke up. He did not have the deep, commanding voice that Ma expected. Instead, it was high, like a woman's voice. Maybe that is why he never spoke in public. He probably could not stand people laughing at him.

"Bolt it, dipshit! I did not ask you to do it. I ordered you hit that guy. When we killed the Chief, they could have run your profile. They did not. You weren't going to jail. We know what the soldiers are here for, and for a while this morning, we knew where every one of them was. The idea was to start a skirmish, draw them out, and see their weapons and training. I can't start killing without knowing what my enemy is capable of. We will need to take their base to stop them from calling for help, and then we will need to kill them all. I still don't know enough. When we do, we shoot them all. But that is later. Right now, we need more."

Sgt. Ma had heard enough. She crept closer to house number two and tried to peek through the windows. She had heard four voices, but five men were inside, and she readily identified both Kahn and Baccus.

The group argued a bit more, and Kahn said, "Ok, I have had it. You guys get out of here. We are going to try for more information tomorrow. We have several dozen bugs in place and will learn from them."

Ma watched three men leave the house, with just Baccus and Kahn still inside. Without hesitation, Ma went to the same door the three men had just left. It had not been able to close yet. She placed a hand on the closing door and ducked quietly inside.

She could not take a direct route to the remaining men. Instead, she took a door to her left and then turned toward the men, walking parallel to them.

They were still arguing, but their voices were lower.

Baccus said, "These soldiers will kill. Since we don't have Planet Militia on this planet, we have gotten by. But, now, the UAS will post sentries and detection devices. How in the hell do you think you can take them?"

Kahn's high voice said, "What is with you? Have you lost your balls? Get with the program, or I will find somebody to take your place. It will be a surprise attack and more coordinated than anything we have done so far. I can give your house and woman to someone else that will earn it."

Sgt. Ma was directly parallel to the two voices, hidden behind a door. She heard both chairs scrape, so she imagined the men were getting to their feet.

She squeezed through the doorway, her weapon hot, with no safety.

Kahn and Baccus saw her and immediately froze. Not just startled by someone in the room with them, but the size of that someone, as she took up most of the space in the room floor to ceiling.

Ma said, "You make a move; I kill you. You scream out for help; I kill you. You beg for your mother, and I kill you. Do you understand?"

Baccus responded first, while Kahn stayed silent.

"Yes. Got it," Baccus said.

Ma indicated with one hand to the floor, "Both of you, on the ground. Do not make a noise. You are dead if even your keys fall out and hit the floor."

Baccus immediately went down, but Kahn was getting his senses back.

"You are the one we recorded the other day. You are bigger than you seemed on camera. Which solar system are you from?" Kahn asked while smiling.

Ma noticed one hand was slipping around his back.

Sgt. Ma politely asked, "Is that a sandwich you are reaching to retrieve? I hope so because whatever you bring out from there, I shove it into your mouth."

Kahn's hand froze.

Ma decided not to take another chance. She hit him in the solar plexus with the tip of the gun. This location has many nerve bundles tied together. If she hit hard enough, Kahn would die.

Kahn doubled over, and Ma used a free hand to squeeze the back of his neck, causing extreme pain. She pushed him onto the floor.

She now had both men down. She pulled her restraint bands from her pocket and neatly bound each pair of hands behind their back. She placed an immobilizer on each man's neck to send 40 thousand volts into the neck muscles on her command. Then, she wrapped tape around each man's head to bind their mouths shut.

"Ok, boys. You each have an immobilizer on your necks. It will hurt like nothing you have ever felt before if you cross me. We have a little walking to do. Up, on your feet." Ma roughly jerked each man to his feet.

She planned to return to her rock, call the base, and ask for transport.

She carried both men to the building's rear with tremendous strength versus the door she had entered.

She had the three of them outside when the shooting started.

"Your people are brilliant. By shooting at me, they are likely to kill you two. You will get on the ground, shoulder to shoulder. I will have one knee each in your backs. Guess what happens if you move?"

Baccus could not help himself. Through his tape, he tried to say, "Got it. We die."

Sgt. Ma returned fire, as she could not only see where the shots came from, but her eyes could make out the gunman.

She shot one man in the chest and the second one in his thigh. Shots were now coming behind her, so she had to spin to get a bead on them.

Ma placed three more shots, and two more men were down.

Ma screamed out, "UAS, I am UAS. I have these two men in my custody. I will kill more of you. You keep firing, and you might kill your friends. Lay down your weapons."

More gunfire erupted and even seemed to be worse. Shots were kicking up dust and rocks all around Sgt. Ma and her prisoners.

One man got close enough to try to stab her from the rear, but she heard him, grabbed his knife hand, pulled him off his feet onto her shoulder, and stood with him. A few of her attackers might see this.

She used one hand to throw the man three meters to the next man coming at her. They both went down in a pile.

Someone else said, "Holy Shit. Did you see the size of that guy? He threw Barney like he was nothing."

As Ma stood, her attackers saw how tall she was.

"Hello, boys. No more of you have to get hurt. You just clear the way. Let me take these two out of here, and everyone can return to bed. Or, you can keep coming, and I will keep killing. You might have noticed I am good at killing. Your serve! 30-love." Ma had no idea why she slipped a tennis phrase into the attack or where she had heard it. But there it was.

The shooting stopped, and the group began to disintegrate into the darkness.

She felt, more than she knew, that the way out of town would likely be people shooting at her back, so she thought to try her communicator.

No signal.

She thumbed an out message to the Captain just in case. The high-pitched and irritating tone told her no connection.

She looked down at her two charges and saw that someone had shot Baccus in his wrist, so she wrapped a field dressing around it.

She got an idea.

She slipped restraint slings below each man's shoulders along his chest, allowing plenty of slack. She picked up Baccus and strapped him over her shoulders, facing the rear. She picked up Kahn with plenty of play and strapped him over her shoulders, facing the front.

Now, whichever direction someone came from, they would see a boss and have to shoot him.

Their combined weight would make her slower and less agile, but she could handle it.

"You guys are my bullet protection. I hope you make it with me tonight. If you don't? Oh, well."

Ma walked out to the central road and began her journey back to her rock. At first, she walked slowly, but as she gained a feel for the men and their weight, she picked up speed. She needed to make a moving target to protect them as much as herself.

A few shots were fired at her legs, but they were all misses, while none shot at the bosses.

The end of the dirt road came soon, and now she was in the town's surrounding area, heading quickly for her rock.

She gained it, lifted the men's straps from her shoulders, and dropped them each unceremoniously on the ground.

She checked her communicator for signal strength and saw it low but present.

She sent the signal for "immediate retrieval, my location."

Then she thumbed a quick message to Captain Redding. "I have the targets. I have taken fire, but we are all ok. Please send transport to me as fast as is possible."

Sgt. Ma again put both men face down, with a knee on each back.

She was facing toward town, waiting.

After a few minutes, she could see a pack of men coming toward her. Two of them had military-style night vision glasses. Since they were only half a kilometer away, she took two shots, splitting each man's night vision and instantly killing them.

As before, mob courage was lost, and the group of men disintegrated and melted back into the town.

Twenty minutes passed before Ma thought she heard a vehicle coming toward her. It was UAS and was a floater, levitating one meter above the ground. It arrived at her location, and two squads of soldiers jumped off, with Captain Redding in the lead.

"Well, Sergeant, what do you have for me?" Redding asked, with a smile as wide as the horizon.

Sgt. Ma said, "Boys, meet my Captain. Captain Redding, meet the two bigshots that have been stirring the peace here. Captain, I do apologize. I had to kill six or so men back in Thinning. I tried not to, but they were determined to kill me."

"Oh, I am sure we can handle it. Are these guys going to be able to talk tonight?" Captain Redding asked.

Ma used one hand on each man's bundle strap and lifted them. "Captain, they have had a rough night. Maybe we let them rest a bit, then ask your questions?"

Redding just could not get the smile off her face. She bent over, looked at the straps, and asked, "Did you have them strapped to you? One in front and the other in the back?"

Ma came to attention and reminded Redding, "Sir, you asked me for plausible deniability and not to get killed. I pulled a rabbit out of my hat. For extra protection, Sir! I am not sure what a rabbit is, but there you are."

Redding had no words. She shook her head and said, "Wow! You are a hell of a soldier."

SIX

Sergeant Ulysses Frederick Grant

Even in kindergarten, all the other children knew Little Freddy as the 'wee' one.

In his growing years of school, male and female classmates grew past him. His shockingly red hair and paper-like pale skin also set him apart from the others.

His lack of height gave him an attitude, as did his name,

"Ulysses Frederick Grant."

He hated Frederick, as frequently somebody would change it to Freddy.

Behind his back, or in groups, the other kids would taunt Little Freddy.

'Little Freddy' sat on him like a stink he could never wash away.

His namesake, the more famous Ulysses S. Grant, was a commanding general in the Civil War and, in 1869, became the 18th President of the original United States on Old Earth.

History labeled Ulysses S. Grant for valor, military tactics, and statesmanship.

Little Freddy was long on courage and guts but short on the other attributes.

Little Freddy would say someone with guts can be too stubborn to give up and likely lacks honor and courage.

He worked with heavy bar weights in his youth to build muscle. He tried to run further and faster than the other kids.

During any sport, his competitive spirit was the strongest on the field.

When he lost, he lost poorly, sulking and hating the winner.

He rubbed it into the competitor's face to prove his superiority when he won.

Little Freddy shielded himself with quick anger, ready to fight anything or anyone, anytime.

Grant was always right even when he was wrong and would get red in the face when challenged. Freddy found fewer people willing to challenge him over the years.

He did not think he was losing friends. Instead, he was proud he had forced them to see his logic with their silence.

Freddy found he enjoyed having no friends in his life. It gave him stature, he believed.

A leader, he thought, surrounded by the lesser crowd.

He joined United Armed Services, barely out of his teens, to show everyone how tough he was.

Promotions came quickly, which probably followed the military formula, "if you can't work with them, promote them the hell out of the way."

He was usually the first to jump off the lander in a battle on any planet, whether wearing a breathing hood or just battle gear. He was not afraid of anyone or anything; he proclaimed to everyone.

When he was first made Sergeant, Grant had a squad of eight soldiers. He drove them more than led them. He volunteered his team for more dangerous jumps than other squads.

He told them openly that his squad would be the meanest, toughest, in all the settled worlds, or they would die.

Some did die or became wounded.

His squad hated Sgt. Little Freddy. The original survivors knew that transferring to another team was difficult, but they tried repeatedly.

His squad of the last three years turned over, one by one, to freshly-minted Space Soldiers filling the spaces left by the old guard.

In his mind, his original squad was soft and hard to direct.

They were 'gutless,' 'softies,' mama's children. The newer soldiers made getting his way more straightforward, as his way was the only way.

One day, Colonel Haskell called Sgt. Grant into his office.

Grant entered, brought his right boot into quick contact with his left boot, and quickly shot his right hand up, thumb tucked behind, just over his right eyebrow.

He knew he looked good with his sharply pleated aquamarine service uniform. Every part of his service uniform that should be shiny was.

He was the poster child for a UAS Space Soldier.

The Colonel began, "At ease, soldier. You might wonder why I asked you in. Well, I have a few purposes. Your squads have had steady complaints since you joined my company and made Sergeant!"

The Colonel noted Sgt. Grant was filling his lungs with air. The Colonel knew he would loudly defend himself.

With both hands quickly extended, he continued, "Now, don't say a word. Because, at this moment, I do not care!"

Sgt. Grant visibly relaxed, though his face's telltale red skin said he was still disturbed and likely angry.

"My next reason for asking you here is to ask you to volunteer for a dangerous assignment! You are the best choice since you never ask for a leave to see family, nor do I ever see you have a friendly beer with others. I have never seen you back down from any battle. So, my assumption is you are comfortable on your own. This mission will be life-threatening."

Sgt. Grant almost smiled and said, "Yes, I will volunteer. Count me in!"

Colonel Haskell paused for a bit and then said, "I knew you would, Sgt."

He paused again, took a tiny breath, and said, "Last, I want you to know that I have chosen a teammate for you that is also comfortable on her own!"

Sgt. Grant's skin started turning red again.

"Her? Is it a woman? Colonel sir, I must protest! With all due respect, I do not feel comfortable putting a female on the front lines. I will have to protect her and remove my attention from any assignment! We might both die! Give me a guy, sir!" Grant was working up a full head of steam.

Grant's protestations seemed to amuse the Colonel, as a hand had quickly moved up to his face to hide his smile.

"Sgt. You will meet her in the next few minutes. You will train with her for the next four days. You will become a team. Your next port of call is Mortson2, an outer planet two solar parsecs from here. A Clarion class starship will get you there quickly, but you will then transfer to a Space Brigade planet ship. That journey will take you almost two weeks. Then, you will take a 3-person lander to the planet. Someone took Trionan Scientists hostage, and the thugs are demanding 40K Tolerans to get them back alive. One has a personnel locator chip embedded in his body. He should be easy to find."

Colonel Haskell let that soak in for a few beats and then continued.

"I expect you and Sgt. Ma, to reconnoiter, find out how many are involved and where the Trionan is. Once you have enough knowledge, you are to dispatch all hostiles with extreme prejudice. Save the Trionans if you can. But destroy all evidence.

And, I mean, all evidence. We must signal these thugs that they cannot hold All World's citizens for ransom. Use your recorder for the occasion. It will make excellent material to keep the animals at bay once broadcast on the news vids."

Again, he paused. "Do you understand, Sgt.? Nod your head, first up, then down if you do!"

Sgt. Little Freddy was seething but knew there was nothing he could do right now. He took a cleansing breath, tried to unclasp his jaw, and said, "Yes, Colonel, I get the picture. The quicker I meet the little lady, the better off we will be. We have a lot of work to do!"

Colonel Haskell could not stop the sudden grin that flew onto his face.

"Well, let's do just that, shall we?" Colonel Haskell turned back to his desk and touched one button on his hologram hovering above his desk to connect his office microphone with the loudspeaker in his outer office.

"Sgt. Ma, come in here, please!"

The door behind Sgt. Grant opened, and as he turned to see what the little lady looked like, he was pretty confused by what was happening in the doorway.

A black form in an aquamarine UAS uniform had bent down to move through the doorway, ensuring that the head and shoulders were low enough and twisted enough to come through the entrance without damaging the door.

As she entered the room, she straightened and, when fully erect, gave a sharp salute to the Colonel, just as Sgt. Grant had earlier.

"Sgt. Ma is reporting for duty, as ordered!"

Colonel Haskell returned the salute and turned to Sgt. Grant to make the introductions.

Colonel Haskell saw Sgt. Grant was spellbound.

Haskell noted that Grant's head barely came to Ma's breast area, his entire body was shaking, and he seemed to be wetting himself.

"Here, here, Sgt. Get control of yourself," Colonel Haskell's command boomed.

Sgt Grant's face seemed to be red enough to put off a glow as he became aware of his wet crotch.

"Well, sir, can I be excused? I, I, I must run to sick call. I believe I must have Perovian bacteria attacking my gut area.

I think I am coming down with something dire. It might be lethal."

Sgt. Grant tried to cover his wet area with his hands and spoke loudly, "Hell, it might be contagious!"

All the time, Sgt. Grant looked almost straight up at Ma while moving towards the door and finding a way around Sgt. Ma, at the safest distance the room provided.

Sgt. Ma watched him maneuver around her with no emotion showing on her face. She was pretty used to Terraens and their reaction upon first meeting her.

However, wetting oneself self was a new one to Sgt. Ma!

Colonel Haskell seemed to contain some convulsion in his stomach with his left hand while his right hand was over his jaw. A jaw clenched so tightly that his lips appeared to be one thin line.

"Yes, Sgt. You go to sick call!"

Finally, Sgt. Grant had made it to the door, opened it, and shot through.

Simultaneously, the Colonel could not contain himself anymore as his laughter burst out.

He did not want to offend Sgt. Ma, as he waved a hand back and forth to her as if to say, “No, I am not laughing at you.”

His laughter evolved into coughing and sputtering, and still, he laughed.

A little calm entered him, and he said, "Well, that is the last time Sgt. Grant will refer to you as 'the little lady,' I think!"

His laughter again threatened to break out, but the Colonel had military training and was determined to keep it in check. He tried to refocus his mind with deep breathing.

All would remember this meeting, though Sgt. Ma likely would have the slightest understanding.

The Colonel was so proud of his tactics and knew he had to put this event in his memoirs, but his laughter burst forth once more at the mere thought of writing it down.

He tried more deep breathing, finally wiped the tears from his eyes, gained his composure, and turned his attention to Sgt. Ma.

"Now, Sgt. Ma, let's you and I discuss what we can do about this situation. I believe that a metal chair will hold your physique. At least, my flight surgeon thought so."

He thought he saw irritation in her face and went on.

"Oh, I do hope I did not insult you, but you Aleutins are taller and denser than Terraens, so I have to cover my bases."

Ma's face seemed to relax a bit.

"Now, rule number one, try not to get so mad at Little Freddy that you could or should squash him like a piss ant! OK? You need him for this mission," Colonel Haskell said and raised his right hand with one finger extended.

"Rule number two is to let him think he is in charge," he said with two fingers. "I have read your file thoroughly; I know how well you can reason with soldiers."

Now there were three fingers. Colonel Haskell said, "Rule three is you will have to bring all of your saboteur knowledge to bear, to save these scientists and destroy everyone else present."

Colonel Haskell was now finished with rules and counting.

He had both hands on his hips and thought it was best to let Sgt.

Ma respond.

"Sgt. Ma, is there anything you want to ask or add?"

Sgt. Ma tried to speak, pulled back, pondered for a few seconds, and asked politely,

"What is a piss ant, Sir?"

SEVEN

Planetfall - I Lost my Love for Flora

Before landing on Mortson2, Sgts, Ma, and Grant were given a historical recording to further their information about Trionans. This background information provided techniques Trionans have used for millennia.

This recording of one historical planet fall will give any listener understanding of why and how we Trionan scientists do what we do.

On the one hand, it appeared to be a colossal failure for me but, in retrospect, gave fruit to a very successful mission.

Our Trionan shuttle landed before sunrise on this rather average-looking planet.

Someone hearing this recording might think it is odd, but Trionans record everything in our lives for future study. My species are primarily analytical, so we have many more scientists than artists.

Landing here was lovely to our group since it had a plethora of land, water, and life.

As we were all stuck in our ship for weeks, it was past time to stretch our tentacles.

My ship's mission is to study, and classify flora, fauna, and life on any planets within our reach. This solar system has one star and nine planets.

Trionans have proudly been peaceful and civilized for more

than a millennium. We are initially from the Polaris Tri-Star system, but many left the homeworld to study others.

Anyone from Trion is blessed with a relatively long-life cycle compared to other Milky Way galaxy species.

Trion is near the center of the Milky Way galaxy, and as a result, our planet has matured many years ahead of the one we landed on in the galaxy's outer bands.

Our system has our yellow supergiant star's gravitational influence on two smaller stars. We have four planets in orbit. The system is approximately 4133 light-years or 133 parsecs from this minor planet we were presently on.

The mother ship was still in orbit, as it had dispatched shuttles to various landmasses, including the frozen north and South poles, near the hotter equators, and examples like this one in a more moderate climate.

My fellow scientists took air, soil, and water samples.

I spent the better part of the morning following a trail of a quadruped herbivore whose primary diet was the local grasses. It left me with flora and fauna. For variety, I collected any animal droppings I found along the way.

This allowed me to collect primary and secondary specimens from animals and flora.

Near where I was recording this collection, I bent to remove an unusual specimen of flora that had prodigiously spread violet petals and a sharply contrasted green stalk.

Sunlight filtered through the trees and made me squint despite my eye visor as I attempted to uproot the plant. Tenacious as its roots were, all my attention was releasing it from the soil without damaging the plant.

Before I could free it, I heard the sound of two bipedal creatures as they crashed through the underbrush and low-lying branches.

When I first spied the two through the woods, she in front and the male specimen in dogged pursuit, I thought I should run.

Then, I assumed they would run past where I crouched under cover of the trees and flowers.

I hid, which is how I became a trapped audience of their youthful passion.

Imagine my surprise when the female turned to her pursuer and grabbed him.

They soon pulled on each other as if to control the others' bodies.

I felt that violence was about to take place.

Gorge rose in my throat at the mere thought of someone or something hurting other living beings.

However, as she was smiling and laughing, I felt that my first impulse regarding violence must have been wrong.

She fell as if her foot had become entangled in a root. As she still had him in her clutches, he had to follow her to the grass.

They were within reaching distance of where I lay hidden.

I didn't think they would appreciate my appearance or presence, and we Trionan have a firm policy of not interfering with any sentient beings.

For this reason, I froze like an Antex fly in amber. My face was close enough to the soil to savor the aroma of plants hovering near my position, teased and tickled by their effect.

Yet, I soon smelled something else, something musky. I decided the bipedal sex glands produced abundant hormones as they pawed over each other's coverings.

She rolled him over, pushed him down, threw her long blond hair over her shoulders, and removed her protective covering.

He stared at her at first in apparent ignorance and then beamed. He, too, removed his clothing, but more quickly.

I distinctly heard his garments as they were hastily rent from his body.

I had been watching them for a time without discovery, but I felt like I was spying.

I could not move away nor reveal myself. In doing so and breaking one of our primary rules, I knew I would receive a firm reprimand from Chief Dr. Harlequit.

More than likely, the Dr. would restrict my reading time as punishment.

So, I lay and recorded their movements and sound.

We had understood that the females of this world were the more passive of the species, but as I watched them, I realized that she was controlling him.

At first, his clumsy moves were too fast to suit her. She spent several minutes calming him and adjusting his eagerness.

There was now a mutual rhythm to their movements, a rocking, while the two's sounds were humorous.

We Trionans have had little need for sex in many centuries. We only use procreation from time to time. Science has replaced it and the processes involved. We have risen above simple animal lust. We need a proper laboratory.

However, as I lay there, listening and observing, I had the most curious sensation.

My libido seemed to wake.

As their rocking and guttural emanations became more animated and faster, I became more excited to my horror.

Just at the climatic sexual moment, when the couple was at their frenzied peak, she said, “Oh God,” several times. He grunted in a most animalistic way.

I found myself standing, pushing on my worlstoy, and heard myself grunt in kind! The passion of my moment passed, and I looked down at them in absolute horror.

They seemed not to have seen me!

She probably thought it was he grunting, and he most assuredly thought it was she.

I was most embarrassed and tried to ease back down to the forest floor without discovery.

They were relaxed now, unlike me.

I felt most revolted by my behavior. The recorder had made a note of all of this. It was against the rules for me to turn it off, or worse, to erase it.

But how could I face my survey commander, Chancellor Gronkint?

How could I look in her eye without thinking of my sordid behavior?

Could I explain this as a runaway emotional state, caught in the heat of the moment? Perhaps I could blame the flora spores for my lack of civilization! An allergic reaction?

That's it! I will blame the flora for affecting me!

Everyone but Dr. Couragionit would believe that! (He wouldn't believe anything unless it came from a computer.)

I am sure I could change the toxicology report to a point where some aberrant behavior patterns could be possible in the Trionan psyche and thus disguise my hideous behavior.

While these thoughts were running through my head, the overheated couple simmered again.

I gathered that once the young male had tasted her fruits by her design, he decided it was his turn to take the initiative.

So they began!

Though their positions had changed, their joint motion soon became as their last.

Soon, I heard the 'Oh God' and the grunts.

This time, I was determined to control my urges. With tremendous self-control, though I had started, I stopped pushing on my worlstoy.

Still, my libido screamed for attention.

I gained more control as they relaxed again.

That was better!

I looked at this planet's one-star position in the sky and realized I needed to leave soon. Attempting to navigate without proper light concerned me as I had seen countryside with steep hills and rocks where I would have difficulty.

But my newly found friends seemed to have nothing better to do than lie in the leaves and mate like two Griniskyintes.

I thought I should make a noise and scare them away. I thought, "I'll throw a rock. They will think someone is coming! They will then leave!"

While I lay planning, the female began manipulating herself with one of her appendages, smiling curiously at her mate.

It appeared as if the male had satisfied his curiosity and his hormones. But the female had decided that she needed a little more.

He shook his head in amazement while she smiled and manipulated.

She pushed him back down onto his back with a most determined set of her jaws. Then her head disappeared from my view.

What was she doing now?

As my curiosity became more robust, I raised just a tiny amount to view them better.

Her head seemed to be at his mid-body level. I couldn't quite see what she was doing.

At first, he seemed to resist. But soon, she erased his resolve and irritation. He became more animated.

She climbed on top of him as if to control or dominate him.

Again the motion was repeated, and the sounds. Also, I felt the pull of my desires.

I became lost this time in the smells and sounds and did not realize what I was doing.

Pushing firmly on my worlstoy, I came more upright. Now, I could see, smell and hear them fully. It was an immersing experience for me.

I knew only that my libido was in control.

She began, 'Oh God! Oh, God!' again.

He began grunting, and this time I felt like I would explode. I felt as I had never felt before. I felt like the cosmos was pulling my essence out of my body. I felt one with the universe.

I heard a deep guttural voice yelling, "Ride me! Ride me, my pink stallion!"

Simultaneously, I heard the female yell, "Oh God!" But her voice sounded very different this time.

As I returned to my senses, I realized that I had yelled the 'Pink Stallion' thing.

I looked down at my bi-pedal friends and realized they looked at me in abject horror.

They would consider me ugly, so different from them with my eight appendages and rounded body and head.

After all, they only have four appendages.

Well, five if you consider the small one the male had.

There they were without their clothing coupling, and I was self-manipulating my worlstoy like a fool!

It would have taken a wise mind to realize who was the most mortified and afraid.

The male bolted with a single reaction, leaving his wrappings and female companion lying on the ground. She was screaming and crying while trying to gather her coverings to shield her body.

Running through the forest did not allow for full speed, but I did the best I could. I left as quickly as I could. I turned and knocked down a small tree in my path.

Running back to the lander, I decided I had to lose that recorder.

I did not need a record of this day. Let them punish me as they will. I will make up some story about an animal scaring me, or perhaps a tree root trip and dropping the 'corder over a mountain's edge, in a running stream, or into a rodent's hole.

I will not have my survey brethren berate me about my performance here for the next two months until we make our next planetfall in the Ulsaxiious Sector. I will be so glad to see a world with three suns again.

As I neared the Shuttle, I slowed my passage and tried to breathe slower.

I needed to compose myself before anyone saw me, and I had to have my story straight about the ‘corder.

However, I intend to experiment with this expression more. The feelings of being one with another are something I wanted to repeat.

My newfound toy, my worlstory, will probably demand it.

Perhaps Chancellor Gronkint might want to meet with me privately.

I think she has touched my appendages a few times with more purpose than I could have given her credit. Perhaps she, too, would want to try these more ancient emotions for herself.

I am attracted to her.

She has a beautiful orange eye that seemed to look into mine on previous occasions.

EIGHT

Take Cover

Sgt. Grant angrily thought the universe was not big enough for him and the big shadow bitch from Aleutin, Sgt. Ma.

Colonel Haskell had forced Sgt. Grant on this mission with the big one, but he had no intention of allowing her to come back alive.

Previously, Sgt. Grant had pissed himself the first time he laid eyes on her and could not understand how his military career could recover from that.

In his mind, she had destroyed his manhood and military career. He had lost everything he cared about because of her.

He had to spend four days training with her to get used to each other's methods.

Every day was a struggle to wake up, get dressed, and go to meet with her. He found he could never look into her eyes without embarrassment and anger.

He saw no way to get his pride and life back unless he killed her.

After spending the journey in hibernation, the two of them had woken three hours before in the Brigade planet plasma ship.

Then they transferred their gear and themselves into this smallish lander. Of course, Ma took up the most room.

Their travel would benefit as the lander was fully automated for safe arrival, just like most modern space crafts were automated.

Larger vessels did have flight crews, but they rarely intervened in the quantum computers' flawless work.

Grant and Ma only needed to know nothing more than coordinates, and someone had already put them into the lander computer system.

In his mind's eye, he imagined booting her out of the lander, still short of planetfall by 50 kilometers.

But he had a feeling that the giantess would survive sudden decompression, entry into the atmosphere, and the sudden stop.

Regardless, he did not understand how to trick her into moving over to the emergency port. Or how to open it before planetfall.

He was unsure if he could muster enough strength to move that big ass outside.

Finally, he was unsure if he would not just fall after her if he achieved all of that.

Damn! And, Double Damn!

He had already tried to suffocate her by removing the filter in her breathing tube and reversing it.

Who knew she could hold her breath for the five frigging minutes it took to take her space military gear off and fix it?

When she shook her head, he knew she thought it was her fault and had installed it wrong.

Damn and double damn!

Triple damn it!

She was an Aleutinite, he a Terraen.

Her skin was as black as coal, and she could touch the ceiling with her head if she wanted.

Neither was correct for him, as he was a pasty white and shorter than the Old Earth average.

In his very soul, he knew Sgt. Ma was superior to him in every way, but Little Freddy never lost, even when he lost.

He would find some way to take her out. His very survival as a real man demanded her death.

The proximity sensors were now calling out the speed of descent and distance to the ground. Radar and thermal imaging automatically followed the coordinates necessary for the safe and correct landing point on Mortson2.

The military's latest intel on this small planet was only five hundred thousand souls of various species, mainly miners.

Grant knew they had a hike in front of them as their landing spot was nowhere near the town but was the best landing spot in the hills that the intel could locate. This way would be safer, as the likelihood of running into aggressive people was less.

Intel stated the air was breathable but had an unpleasant metallic smell and taste. This rock was helpful for many types of minerals and salts.

Mining companies had built a healthy economy, sending mined material off-planet, trading for things missing in the local economy, like foodstuff, medical supplies, and water. Nothing edible grew here for various reasons, including low rainfall, but the air and soil likely did not encourage the foothold necessary for life.

Grant could understand taking a scientist hostage. But who did the idiots think would pay them?

A few minutes passed when the proximity alarms sounded, showing immediate planetfall.

The vibration of the lander had now become somewhat unpleasant to Sgt. Grant. He glanced at Ma and guessed she must be asleep.

Of course, she was. Nothing seemed to bother the big bitch.

Touchdown took place.

The lander went through its automatic functions to put

everything safely asleep that would not be needed here on the planet, ready to awaken again when its personnel was required to get back into space.

Sgt. Ma was catlike as she was immediately awake, removing her body restraints and standing up while grabbing her gear with one hand.

Sgt. Grant was slower as his body had not adjusted to the gravity or lack of vibration. He found himself slightly nauseated.

But he stubbornly did the same as Ma and followed her out of the open lander portal. Three steps down, and they were on a somewhat yellowish surface. The soil here was very sandy, with a mixture of coarse and fine sand. Sgt. Grant noticed that Ma was leaving giant footprints, and a cloud followed her.

Grant got an idea and then rejected it. Military superiors could easily trace the firing of military weapons. Shooting her in the back would gain him nothing but his execution.

Instead, he caught up to her and whipped out his location equipment to show their present position in a blue dot, while the Trionan scientist would show in red.

Sgt. Grant said, "We go this way!" while pointing left with his arm.

The two had to adjust their paths slightly by turning slightly to their left. They had taken only five steps when shots rang out, and they both fell to the ground.

"Who in the hell is shooting at the UAS? Halt! Identify yourself! Stop shooting. We are United Armed Services!" Sgt. Grant yelled out.

Both soldiers were prone in the sand but looking in the direction from which the shots came.

More shots came in and raised yellowish clouds in front of them.

Sgt. Ma knew what to do but waited to give Sgt. Grant time to get his orders together, letting him lead as Colonel Haskell ordered.

"Ma, you low crawl over to the rock on your left while I get their attention and fire. I will run to that tree over there. That will give you time to sight them in and kill them."

Grant gained his feet and ran for the tree, with enemy fire following his steps.

Sgt. Ma stayed low and crawled to the rock outcropping. She spotted the muzzle fire from the enemy. She could have lobbed a grenade and taken them out, but she preferred to see who it was.

She made an arc away from the kill zone and came in behind the shooters. She could hear Sgt. Grant bellowing orders to no one while returning fire in a blatant attempt to keep the fire trained on himself.

Ma thought, "He is no coward. He is courageous if foolhardy!'

Sgt. Ma found the position and was surprised to find an unmanned automatic gun placement with infrared and sonar positioning equipment.

These were like the rifles she and Grant carried. They were particle weapons, using electromagnetics to accelerate a particle to ultra-high speeds.

She found the electrical circuit and flipped the switch off. The gun placement was now safe.

Ma got up on a rock, waved her hands, and keyed her radio for Grant, "Clear to advance. It is an automatic gun placement. I turned it off."

Sgt. Grant stayed near the trees but quickly covered the ground to where she was. When he arrived, Ma pointed at it and said, "Someone was ready for incoming personnel and wanted to stop them here."

Sgt. Grant looked at the equipment, raised his rifle, and gave a short three-round burst into the "brains."

"You might realize I had deactivated the gun?" Ma asked.

Grant glared at her, “Well, I killed it. No more worries.”

Grant turned the other way, pulled up his locater, making sure their direction was right, and said, “Let’s go.”

The two of them resumed their field march in the scientist's direction.

Everything on this planet or planetoid seemed to have strange colors. The vegetation that existed seemed short, and the colors were wrong. What would appear to be a tall bush or short tree did not have green leaves but tended towards yellowish. Smaller growth had flower-like petals with a diversity of shades of yellow and orange.

To Grant, it was just bizarre. Ma did not consider it, as she had seen similar and worse in her travels.

Sgt. Grant kept moving them to higher ground, where the ground cover was sparse.

Ma knew this was the incorrect way to proceed, but she followed the Colonel’s orders by letting him lead.

The high ground made them easy to see and pick off if there were sharpshooters in the area.

They had field marched some five klicks when gunfire rang out again, but this time it came from three different compass positions. Some shots came very close.

The two were on their bellies for the second time in less than an hour.

Ma again waited on Sgt. Grant, though again, she knew what to do.

Grant took his time, considered his options, and said, “Ok, we split up again. You to the left, and try to get that bastard, I will go to the right and get that one. And, dammit, even if it is an automatic robot, kill the damn thing, Sgt.”

Ma nodded and crawled to her left till she could gain cover. While she was moving, she thought she heard something overhead.

She bet it was a hovering object with positioning equipment and likely a camera. It was easy for her to get a bead on it and blow it out of the sky.

The drone fell to the ground, and the gunfire closest to her stopped.

Now she knew what she would see.

She looked to the right into the sky and saw another drone circling over Sgt. Grant's head. He had drawn some heavy fire and was undercover.

Ma shot that drone out of the sky, and that gun placement also quit firing.

Ma performed her arc again, expecting another automatic placement.

Instead, she found a short, skinny being covering that final gun position while staring at computer screens that were likely drone-produced.

She crept up behind him and jerked him from the ground, his feet dangling while the dust clinging to his clothes and feet drifted to the ground.

He was somewhat humanoid, but his eye placement was too wide to be from Old Earth. The shape of his head was incorrect, as well. His hair was a light brown and relatively coarse, as the individual strands were more string than hair.

Sgt. Ma did not know the language the being was speaking. Though he tried to hit her, he missed her body by a large margin hanging the way he was.

"Sgt. Grant, all clear. Come and see what I have found!" Ma said as she keyed her radio.

Grant once again covered the distance while staying close to cover.

He saw the being at the end of her arm and screamed at her, "What are you doing? I told you to kill it, not play with it!"

Sgt. Grant came closer to the being and asked the same questions, over and over, "Who are you? Why are you trying to kill us? Where did you come from?"

Every time the little man attempted to answer, his responses made no sense.

Every time, Sgt. Grant upped the volume in his voice.

Ma said, "Perhaps we let him down and follow him back to his town or teammates?"

Grant said, "No, I will kill him."

The being became very agitated, and Ma said, "Even though we cannot understand him, he can understand us. Let's try to reason with him."

Grant did not like the idea but thought it might be handy if they had a hostage. "Go ahead. Waste your time. I will sit over there in the shade while you communicate with the turd."

Sgt. Ma still had the skinny one in the air but looked at Grant and asked, "What is a turd?"

Grant had already turned his back and waved a hand while moving ever closer to the shade.

Ma turned the being to look at her and spoke simply, "I do not know why you tried to shoot us, but you can see we are well trained. My partner wants to kill you. I do not. If you cooperate with us, he will not have the excuse to kill you. Do you understand? Do you know Universal English?"

The being shook his head to the positive and seemed a bit calmer. He spoke slowly in Universal English to respond, "I understand. I understand more than I can speak."

"Ok. I will put you back on your feet, but we will have to shoot you if you try to run. If you move towards the gun, we will have to shoot you. Do you understand that?"

"Yes, I do. My name is Benzil," He said.

"Good, Benzil. Your accent is strange. What is your home planet? Speak slowly, and I think I can understand you. Sgt. Grant might not, but I think I will. I am Sgt. Ma. First, do you know of a Trionan scientist that came here over five weeks ago?"

Benzil said, "Yes. He and his team came here to take samples from this world. And I am from Grinisky."

Sgt. Ma glanced at Grant, but he did not return her look.

"Benzil, can you tell me what happened to the team and the scientist?" Ma asked.

At first, he looked at his bare feet, and Ma noticed he had odd-shaped feet, with only a big toe. Where the other toes would be was more of a singular bone. His feet seem better suited to sand than soil.

"Yes, I know. A group of us thought it would be easy money to hold the scientists hostage and negotiate money for their return. We are only miners here, and most of us have little to eat. We are supposed to get a fair exchange for the things we mine, but our company seems to forget about food and water. A nearby world, Chapman, will supply us with food and water, but it is expensive, and they will not trade for our minerals. They want All World's currency," Benzil said. "We don't trust them at all."

"Ok, that makes sense. Why did you try to kill us with automatic weapons?" Sgt. Ma asked.

Benzil now looked directly in her face, "Well, we are not soldiers, and we don't have many among us that know weapons. The robotic defense is the best we have. My father knew the hostage-taker group was wrong. He knew someone would come to free the scientists. He thought whoever would try to kill all of us. We were just supposed to scare you off if we could. His shift is at nighttime, and I have the daylight. We have been here for five days now, waiting. My father and I are not part of the hostage-takers. We just want to live in peace and mine the minerals."

Ma glanced again at Sgt. Grant hoped he was listening to this, but his eyes were closed, and he seemed to ignore their conversation.

Ma asked, “Where is your father, then? We will not hurt him if he does not try to hurt us.”

Benzil looked back at the rock outcropping where Grant was seated and pointed that way. “My father is in the small cave, just to one side of where your partner is. With all the gunfire, I doubt he will come out without me calling to him.”

He pointed to the hole, and suddenly Sgt. Grant stood up, strolling to the opening with his gun at the ready and its safety off.

Ma picked up Benzil with one hand and ran to the opening while blocking Sgt. Grant from progressing further.

She set Benzil down and told him, “Call out to your father,”

She glanced at Grant; from his sudden redden skin, she knew he was angry with her.

Benzil began in his language to call his father out.

It seemed to take a long time but was likely only a few minutes when an older version of Benzil slowly popped his head out from inside the cave. He seemed confused, but she knew he was frightened.

She motioned for him to come on out, and he took two tentative steps to make it outside into the light.

“Does your father speak Universal?” Ma asked.

Benzil shook his head, “No, he does not. I will have to translate if you speak slowly.“

Ma said, “Well, tell him we will not hurt him or you. We only want to free the hostages. I need you both to show us where they are kept. The hostage-takers are another story because some will get hurt if they do not give up on the scientists! We have orders to kill them.” Ma stated.

Sgt. Grant glared at her and said, "You are damned straight we will hurt the hostage-takers. And, Ma, you had better not get in my way again. I will not give you another warning!"

Ma looked back at him and said, "We need info, and we can get it from these two. If they are dead, there will be nothing to learn."

Grant grunted, dropped his gun barrel to point at the ground, turned around, and returned to the shade.

Ma looked back at Benzil and said, "Tell your father what I said."

Benzil spoke, and his father looked from Ma to Grant, then pointed at Grant and said something. Benzil shook his head in agreement and talked more, apparently calming him down.

Then Benzil turned back to Sgt. Ma and said, "He understands and agrees. We will take you to them. I doubt you can talk them out of the hostages, though. Everyone is hungry, and there is not much hope of that changing."

Sgt. Grant said from his shaded place, "I can't understand what you are saying, but it sounds like you will guide us. Let me have Benzil up here in the lead. The older man behind him and the two of us make up the rearguard. If there is any shooting, they get it first."

The young man followed orders. He motioned his father to fall in behind him. Grant went next, with Ma trailing.

Ma noticed that Grant did not have his safety on his particle rifle. He wanted to kill something and would likely do so at the first excuse. Moving prisoners with a loaded weapons off safe was against UAS protocol.

The four of them marched into the setting sun, with the ground rising in front of them. Their only change to their direction was to avoid obstacles.

Along the way, various ground creatures skittered away from them.

Sgt. Ma asked, "Are there any dangerous creatures on this

planet?"

Benzil turned his head to reply, "No, there are not. Not even insects. Unless you are mining, it is a very boring place to be."

NINE

Townies

The small band walked for another three hours as Sgt. Grant kept a close eye on the locater.

Though Ma could see, she doubted anyone else could as the sun approached the horizon.

She knew they must stop for the group's safety and that Grant would have to make the call.

The older man stumbled over a rock, fell to the ground, and tumbled partway down the slope. Sgt. Grant made no move to help him.

Benzil chased his father down the slope and now helped him stand again.

Grant whispered, "Let's find a flat place big enough for all of us. Ma, get those restraints out of your field pack. We will bind the old man to Benzil and me to you."

Sgt. Ma nodded in the dark and said, "That is a good idea."

In reality, she thought it was a stupid idea. The older man was going nowhere in the dark, Benzil would stay with his father, and if somebody attacked, none of them could maneuver easily.

But she did as he ordered once they found a relatively flat area. The restraints required her code to open and close, so she entered it twice.

Sgt. Ma thought this world strange, as there did not seem to be any night sounds from insects, animals, or anything else. The quiet of the night was disturbing, while the dark was forbidding.

Sgt. Grant did not get much sleep as he was too worried about getting attacked. His two charges seemed to settle in and rest, though he had no way of knowing they slept, nor did he care. With disdain, he noticed how easily Ma went to sleep.

Grant did finally let the night take him and slumbered.

Slowly, Mortson2's red sun crept over the hills and chased the night away.

Ma nudged Grant's foot while looming over him.

Sgt. Grant said, "Damn you, I just drifted off to sleep a short time ago. But we do need to get going."

Grant jumped to his feet and hollered at his two prisoners, "On your feet, let's get it." He checked the personal locater direction and saw they were still on track.

Sgt. Grant asked Benzil, "How much further?"

Benzil answered, but Grant could not understand his thick accent, so he turned to Sgt. Ma.

Ma said, "We should reach them by early afternoon, he said."

Ma opened her field pack and shared some filling military rations to give them calories for another day of walking.

Sgt. Grant said, "Prepare to break camp. We need to move."

Without another word, Grant shoved the older man in the correct direction. He waved his hands at his son to carry on with the journey.

The four began their march and did not stop for a few hours.

Benzil showed they would be safe near an outcropping of rocks, protected from sight, and there was a small watering hole where they could replenish their canteens.

Benzil noticed that every time Grant looked at Ma, there seemed to be a mixture of anger and disgust. As he knew Grant did not understand much of what he said, he asked, "Why are you two together? He does not seem to trust you much."

Ma smiled at that. She thought it was thoughtful of Benzil to capture the situation correctly. She said, "Well, I am not what the Sgt. would expect of a soldier, but I assure you we partner well."

Benzil shook his head, doubting that was true. He saw them as opposites, and it went beyond the color of their skin or their sizes.

Sgt. Ma was calm. Grant seemed wrapped with intenseness.

Ma seemed to have compassion, which was an obvious hole for Grant.

Though Ma seemed to follow Grant, Benzil doubted that that should be the case.

"Ok, troops, back to the march. Let's go!" Grant hollered, and again they began.

Two more hours passed into the late afternoon when Benzil stopped just below the rise. Sgt. Ma approached him and asked, "Why did you stop?"

Benzil said, "If you look over that ridge and down, you will see our township. There are about 100 people there, in 30 houses. You will see we have no cover getting down to the town. If you want to sneak into town, I suggest you wait until nightfall."

Sgt. Ma explained the translation to Grant, turned back to Benzil, and said, "Thank you. It is Sgt. Grant's decision, but I agree to wait till night is the best."

Grant heard the exchange and got irritated at her, but he knew she was right.

Instead Sgt. Grant said, "Ok, let's find someplace to camp for the night. I will take a peek with the range glasses and see if there are some weak points we need to know about the town."

Sgt. Grant lay on the dirt, with only his range glasses and part of his head above the ridgeline. He scanned the houses, looking for activity, but he saw little movement aside from a few people moving back and forth.

And he verified Benzil's thought. Somebody would see their small group if they tried to go into town during the daylight hours.

He scrambled away from the rise and said to Sgt. Ma, "It will be dark soon. There is not so much as a scrub brush we can hide behind. We will wait till about a few hours before the sun comes up and go into the town. Let's grab some shuteye. Same as last night, I bind the old man to me. You tie Benzil to you."

Sgt. Ma just nodded and did as ordered. While she was restraining Benzil, she asked, "Do you know where in town the scientists likely are?"

Benzil nodded his head to the affirmative, "Yes, there is a larger house in the center of town. It is used as a meeting hall and is the only one painted blue. When my father and I left, that is where the scientists were."

TEN

Contact

Ma again woke Sgt. Grant and the others. From a repeat of yesterday, they shared military rations and water and made plans.

She noted that Benzil and his father seemed to need more and slipped part of her MREs into their hands while her back turned to Sgt. Grant.

Sgt. Ma told Grant of the house Benzil had spoken of and its location.

By this time, she had developed a habit of trying to go downslope or to find a depression so she could look him more in the eyes to lower his tensions towards her. She knew he hated his height.

Sgt. Grant said, "I don't believe I can trust our two teammates to come with us or stay here unless we bind them. We can maneuver better without them. So, we leave them in the shade, with food and water, but restrained."

Ma said, "That is agreeable, but neither of us speaks the language. Maybe, we leave Benzil's father here, but take Benzil with us."

Grant waved her off, "No, I have decided. Tie them together, and leave the water and food. They can get by until we get back to free them."

Benzil started to protest but felt Grant would turn his anger to him, so he quieted himself.

Both Sergeants went over the rise in the dark and began their descent. They noticed none of the houses had lights on, so if they were quiet, they should be able to infiltrate the town and trek over to the light blue house.

The first rays of dawn had begun when they approached the closest house. They crept forward, keeping their gear and feet as quiet as possible.

They were only 100 meters from where the light blue house should be from what they could tell in the predawn darkness.

Suddenly, there were sounds of explosions in the distance. Ma guessed it was coming from the township's other side, opposite their position.

Small field explosions began as if from hand-held grenade launchers. Though neither could see the other perimeter of the town, Ma guessed houses on that side were the targets.

There was also hand-held gunfire waking the township up. Targets would have presented themselves during the explosions.

Grant and Ma were lying down when Grant asked, “What in the hell?”

Sgt. Ma said, “Remember these people tried to deal with the Chapman world to buy food. They might have told those people about the scientists, and now they are attacking to get the scientists for themselves! We need to get to that house before the Chapman soldiers do!”

Grant nodded his head and said, “Follow me!” Since he seemed to go in the correct direction, Ma followed. It only took a minute to arrive at the building.

Grant peeped through one window and saw a group of beings huddled in one darkened corner while three men were opposite them looking out of the structure toward the explosions. One had a rifle, and the other two had knives.

Grant said, “Ok, we break in, kill the three, and get the scientists out of there before the mob hits."

Ma said, "I can handle these three easily without firing a shot. After all, the Chapman attackers likely do not know what house the scientists are in, so let's not draw attention here. If you were to take a more forward position, you could pick off the lead elements of the attacking soldiers, and I could extricate the scientists."

ELEVEN

Attack

Grant looked at her, and she knew his blood lust was up. He wanted to kill something.

He said, “Ok, you get the scientists.”

With that, he ran to the opposite side to pick a position where he could kill the attackers.

Sgt. Ma would give the inside team a chance to surrender. She hoped someone understood Universal.

She spoke very slowly.

“I am from UAS. Your town is under attack. You need to protect your loved ones. Let me have the scientists, and you go to protect your families!”

A few minutes passed; she could hear a heated but quiet discussion behind the closed door.

The door cracked open, and the two with knives ran out, but she could tell the one with the rifle was determined to stay.

She backed away from the door, peeked into the window, and saw where he was located.

She moved slightly away from the window, decided on what angle her body should be in for maximum penetration through the window, and then she jumped through as cleanly as she could.

The window frame did not give up without groaning and

breaking wood, as it was not wide enough to allow her entire passage.

Still, she made it inside, and when she stood, the little man with the gun seemed frozen in place.

She imagined he had never seen a being as tall as she. She quickly took his weapon from his quivering hands and told him to run to his family.

He did.

The scientists were excited and scared to see a tall bipedal specimen in the room.

Because of the darkness inside the room, they could mostly see her large dark form, aquamarine uniform, and bright eyes.

She held out both arms towards them, hands down, to show they should get low, and in a whisper said, "I am here to help. They sent the UAS to remove and protect you, Trionans. Get low to the floor, and do not make a sound."

The group followed her orders, and Ma asked, "I count 5 of you. Is that all?"

One of the "scientists" spoke in Universal English with a wonderfully clear voice, "Yes, we are all here."

Ma could not help but notice the creatures seemed related to the species octopus on Old Earth she had seen in her studies. The word's etymology is more Greek than Latin, as it stemmed from Greek pous, for the foot, and Oct for eight.

These beings had the same eight tentacled arms or feet and ample body and heads. But, Ma also noticed they differed from Old Earth Octopi in that they only had one eye, as opposed to the two eyes of octopi she had studied. The ones found on earth had three hearts and maintained very high blood pressure. The Old Earth octopus had the highest brain-to-weight ratio of any invertebrate there, and she reasoned these creatures were similar.

She also knew from her studies of Old Earth that the scientists could not readily account for why the octopus was on Earth, as it did not fit in with any of the theories of how life developed there.

"I wonder if you folks are related to the ones on Old Earth?" she asked but had already spun away from them. For a brief second, she imagined an ancient Trionan ship crashing into the Earth's oceans, with stranded survivors adding their DNA to Old Earth.

Ma positioned at the window nearest the attacking mob.

She triggered her radio three times, such that Grant would know she was successful. She hoped he would fall back to her position to strengthen it.

As agreed in their prior training, she saw Grant coming back to her. He took a clear line of sight, using the building for protection.

Just a few minutes passed as the explosions and gunfire got closer.

As the rising sun illuminated the kill zone, any potential targets would soon be in view.

But what came out between the houses appeared to be android soldiers sent on a kill mission.

Ma knew before her time frame that android manufacturers made them look similar to humans.

Yet, no matter how close the manufacturers came to mimicking humans, less of humanity accepted them.

Circa the 23rd century, government mandates limited both intelligence and appearance. In essence, the mandates dictated that it would be easy to spot an android.

The device's intelligence had to be focused on the work or the task the manufacturer built the android to perform. A cleaning android was concentrated in washing windows, floors, etc., and nothing else. A robot designed to work in wood had most of its artificial intelligence focused on wood.

Sgt. Ma knew from a distance she was staring at androids designed to be soldiers, capable of killing, but directed by human intelligence. They could not kill unless programmed for targets and given the go command. Their collective features were humanoid but frozen expressionlessly. Ma knew these androids had infra-red and radar proximity sensors.

They would easily find the scientists if they got past Ma and Grant.

Each "soldier" carried quite daunting firepower with particle beam rifles, laser pistols, and various small grenades and missiles.

Sgt. Grant was disgusted, "Shit. The Chapmans don't even have the guts to come themselves. Ma, open fire!"

The two laid down murderous fire with combined particle weapons and 48-millimeter grenades.

Though the initial attacking facsimile soldiers were a dozen, five now lay still on the ground, smoke coming outside some of their corrupted bodies.

The others continued to march forward while splitting their firepower between Ma and Grant.

Ma noticed that headshots did not seem as effective stopping them as a shot to the stomach.

"Grant. Go for the navel area." Sgt. Ma called to her partner. "Stop shooting at their heads."

Ma came outside the meeting hall to stand with Grant, and the two continued to fire at every moving target as several dozen shots came their way.

Ma respected Grant as with a minimum of cover, he did not move backward one meter while heavy fire splintered wood near his head and shoulders.

The android soldiers fired explosives, but not directly at the two of them, but to the right and left, which meant they were not only on a search mission but also one of destruction.

Meanwhile, remembering her lessons a few days ago, Ma swept the sky looking for drones. There were several. She let Grant take care of the ground soldiers while she tried to clear the skies, firing first at one target, then the next, then the next.

Sgt. Grant said, "Keep killing them. More are coming up behind."

But Ma noticed that every time a drone came down, things seemed to calm a bit more.

Grant said, "Cover me. I am going to charge."

Ma tried to tell him no, but he was already running forward.

Ma now had to take her attention away from the skies to try to clear a path for Grant to protect him.

He got hit and went down, as one leg was thrown behind him, forcing him to fall.

His head was only down for a split second before he had raised back up to keep returning fire. He took out two more soldiers with excellent naval shots.

Though they did not go down immediately, they slowed down.

Ma ran to him, still delivering fire to the advancing "soldiers," and picked Grant up by his trail pack with one free hand.

She reversed her path by walking backward as she could while still delivering fire.

Since she had picked Grant up facing the same direction, he returned fire as if some robot had never wounded him.

Even in this position, the two UAS took out four more of the enemy.

Ma kicked open the door to the meeting hall and ran to the window.

She asked the scientists, "Do any of you know first aid?"

She tried to throw Grant back towards the scientists but was not surprised when he crawled back to the door and continued to lay down fire.

Since Grant was picking point again, she turned some attention back to the skies but noticed the overhead surveillance kept a safer distance away from the fight.

There were clumps of "soldiers" lying on the ground, and finally, the last one stopped as if someone had switched his fuel off just as he exited the house line.

Ma told Grant, "Cover me. One of you scientists come to check the Sgt. here and see if you can stop his blood loss. It looks like he got hit in his right thigh and shoulder but check him for more damage."

Ma slipped out of the door as Grant hollered at her, "Kill everything in sight."

She ran to the nearest house for cover. She could not hear or see any more drones.

Still, she felt there were more troops.

She low crawled up to the next house and the following one.

Further out, she noticed a clump of individuals, not androids, standing in a ruined mess of a detonated house.

Two beings were behind them with weapons pointed at them.

An amplified voice rang out, "Whoever you are, come out, or we will kill these four. Do it quickly."

Ma thought she could work behind them, so she low crawled in an arc to come in from behind.

"Ok, here is the first one!" the soldier said.

She was only five meters away when the first shot went off, and one hostage collapsed on the ground.

She stood and charged, her long legs covering the ground twice as fast as Sgt. Grant might have done.

One soldier turned his body and gun and pulled the trigger. But Ma was already there. She caught the man's helmet and jerked back with her right hand, which broke his neck.

The other man tried to turn his gun, but Ma drove her knee

upwards into his chest, her blow pushing him high into the air. While she watched, he died of a massive internal wound to his chest and heart, blood spilling inside his body before his body hit the ground with a sickening splat.

The three left were two females and one child. The one on the ground must have been their father and husband, as all three immediately went to his body.

Sgt. Ma said, "I am here with the UAS. You must come with me so I can protect you. There will be time for your loved one later, but not now."

Ma bent over and picked the oldest female, then the younger one, to her feet. The child bounced up by itself and launched into her free arm. Ma quickly handled the crying child and motioned for the sobbing females which way to go.

While all four were moving back to the meeting hall, Ma walked backward, scanning for soldiers or drones.

When the group reached the last house before the meeting hall, Ma signaled Sgt. Grant by thumbing her radio key three times.

TWELVE

Regroup

Sgt. Ma opened the door for her charges and searched for Grant.

He had lost plenty of blood on the floor, but one scientist hovering over him had made a tourniquet for him to slow the bleeding.

He also had a field dressing on the opposite arm and one in the stomach area.

Ma waited, hoping someone would speak and tell her Grant would be ok.

One of the Trionans spoke up, "He just passed out, just as you opened the door. We believe he was holding on, just waiting for you. He lost a lot of blood and will need a transfusion. But, if I understand your physiology correctly, I think he will make it. I am sorry, but I am not used to red blood. I had to fight nausea to carry out these simple measures."

He glanced at the beings huddled around Ma and asked, "Are these the only survivors?"

Sgt. Ma still held the young child and lowered it to the floor, where it reached its mother. "I don't know. Two Chapmans held them hostage, killed the father, and I killed the two of them. I need to perform a sweep of the area, but with Sgt. Grant unconscious that is just not wise. So, instead, I will be on guard here. I hope my communicator can contact our lander. Via the lander, I can contact the UAS. Our lander is too small to get everyone out. I will have to call for a larger lander, which might take a few weeks."

With the situation somewhat stable, Ma now felt she needed to start communications, risking discovery from whoever was out there.

She keyed the highest power and frequency available to her, fearing she was just beyond the range of the lander. She was. It failed with a high-pitched sound. She tried a few more times, with the same results.

So now, Sgt. Ma had a series of problems. Grant was not available to assist and could die. She could not sweep the area and go to a higher altitude to contact the lander.

All because she now had to protect eight souls and perhaps more.

She dug inside her field pack for a drone that would only operate on its stored charge for an hour. And it only had a camera, no weapons. But it was small, easily hidden from the ground, and would beam back images from the kill zone.

She removed her pack and shifted things aside until she found the little black plastic enclosure.

She opened it, and there was the unit about one millimeter wide and thick. Next to it was a plug-in unit that would connect with her field support unit on her body. She could then rotate a unique lens in front of her eye and control the drone and camera flight via voice commands.

She went to the window and executed the voice command to turn on the drone, at which point it rose from her hand and went through the window while rising.

She was satisfied that the camera and her viewing lens were functional, so she sent it out to the battlefield, performing a series of S patterns to cover more area.

From her display, she saw three dozen bodies lying. Somebody had piled several on top of each other.

The drone covered a blank area from there until she found the house where the Chapmans had executed one friendly, and she had executed two hostiles.

They lay as she left them. She momentarily wished there were animals to tear them apart into bite-sized pieces.

Via her voice commands, she ordered the drones to continue from that traveling point to the burned-out house.

She looked for friendly survivors along the way but was stunned by how many bodies lay on the ground. Many were missing limbs from explosions. Others simply shot to bleed out.

As she scanned the area, she saw some living beings. She thought there were maybe 20 survivors in various states of distress. Some were lying on the ground, a few upright. She noted the healthy friendlies were tending to the wounded.

There had to be a Chapman ship, and it had to be large enough for all these soldiers to make planetfall from Chapman.

The drone flew away from the town, but Sgt. Ma thought she saw a sparkle to the left and turned the drone to see what it was.

Though partially hidden at ground level by a small hill, the drone found the troop carrier.

There was no personnel around it, so she flew the drone closer to the ground and the ship to inspect it better.

The lander portal door was open, so she slowed the drone down and changed directions such that it would come from the rear, around its fuselage, and approach the personal portal.

She took the drone to the very top of the portal and slowly entered it.

There was no one inside. All had gone to battle the friendlies, it would seem.

Though she had not seen any more Chapman soldiers, she could not be sure. She hoped they were all dead.

She gave the drone the command to return to her hand and watched the camera to see how the ground forces were fairing.

The drone returned to her hand; she executed the off command and placed it and the plug-in support unit back into the plastic case.

A groan came from Grant, and Ma went to him. "Man, I am dizzy. What is our status Sgt. Ma?"

Ma looked at him carefully to see if he would stay alert for a few minutes.

Sgt. Ma began, "We have succeeded in freeing the Trionan scientists. One helped you stay alive. You and I destroyed some three dozen android soldiers. I found four living friendlies about to be killed by two living hostiles in a sweep of the immediate area. I removed the hostiles after they killed one friendly. I just completed a sweep of the area and could not find any functional or living hostiles. I hope there are no more. I found their troopship. However, from this distance, I cannot contact our lander, so we cannot contact our UAS brigade. So, we are on our own."

"And, you did not get a scratch," Sgt. Grant said, but not in an angry way.

Ma had not thought about it, took off some of her protective military gear, and found several bleeding wounds, but none in areas of concern.

"I believe I will live." Ma said.

Sgt. Grant grunted. He was probably in contempt or jealousy, as he saw the number of wounds she had, yet she was still upright.

The Trionan scientist that had helped Grant moved to Ma and looked over her body. Her face had several abrasions and contusions from her multiple contacts. One arm had been hit with something heavy, likely thrown via an explosive.

There was one deep scratch along the ridge of one shoulder where likely a particle weapon had just grazed her. There were several small holes where he thought they had shot her.

The scientist marveled at the size and apparent strength of this being. He wondered what kind of planet she came from where walking into death and coming out slightly touched was typical.

Grant said, "You know, we left those two Griniskyinites up on the hill. I am sure they are okay, but you probably need to free them and try contacting the UAS base while you are there."

Sgt. Ma mulled this over and said, "If I do that, I leave you all here without protection."

Grant grunted, "Shit. I don't need you here!" He rolled over, grabbed his gun, crawled to the window, used the window ledge to pull himself up, and cocked the rifle while checking the charge levels.

"Sgt. Ma, take off. We will stay here. You know what you need to do."

Ma knew he meant well but was unsure how long he could hold on. She looked around, found something resembling a chair, and took it over to Grant. "Sit here. You can still see someone coming."

She turned to the Trionans and said, "Get some of his rations from his field pack. There are two energy supplements in there. Get him to eat one now with water. The other one, make sure he eats in one hour. It will probably take me twice to go out and come back."

Sgt. Ma gave one final look around the room at the people huddled in fear, one more look at Grant, and immediately went through the door.

She would never have done this before Grant, but she set off on a run rather than a field march. Her long legs could eat up distance much faster than a mere Terraen.

THIRTEEN

Radio

When she arrived at the rise where the two Griniskys were, she was pleased they were still alive, and they seemed delighted she had returned.

Benzil said, "We heard all the explosions and gunfire. Both of us feared you two had died."

Ma bent down to use her code to remove their restraints.

"Where is Sgt. Grant?" Benzil asked.

Ma said, "He is ok for now, but I have to get us to help quickly. Your people were not the problem, but that nearby world Chapman was. They sent an invading force of androids to take your scientists. One of you must have told them that is where you expected the money to come from, and they thought that was a great idea." She swung her field pack down and dug for the communicator for the lander.

"Benzil, I see neither of you touched your water or field rations. You will be weak if you do not partake of it," Ma said.

Benzil said, "We did not know when or if you two would return, so we would space out the time we ate."

Sgt. Ma said, "That is smart, but the two of you eat now. You will need your strength." She watched as they ate, then turned back to where the lander was.

She keyed up the signal and punched in her encrypted code

to get communication started. The high-frequency warbling started, ran a sequence, and connected.

Next, she had to punch another encryption code to get the lander communicator to start the subspace frequencies to hit a UAS receiver.

The frequencies had to sweep, as planet alignment here to there would have to be almost exact unless she caught a UAS fleet ship in between. She lay the communicator on a rock and went back to the Griniskyinites.

Ma knew it was a long shot, but she had no choice but to wait for a connection.

She sat down to rest her body. Some 15 minutes passed when she was startled awake by the confirmation tones.

She went near her communicator to wait, as it carried all the information the other end would need.

"Gunnery Sgt. Alonus Wilson here, UAS plasma ship, Tesla. Over." the other asked.

"Yes, gunnie. I am Sgt. Ma. I assume we caught a bounce from a UAS ship. We are on Mortson2. What is your location? Over." Ma asked.

"The Captain would better answer that question. My navigational skills are poor. But, from the strength of your signal, I bet we are relatively near you. What can I pass along to Captain Billings? What is your need? Over."

"Thank you, gunnie. Ok, short run down. Five Trionan scientists were captured here on Mortson2 by local Griniskyinites. They wanted a ransom paid so they could buy food from the nearby planet Chapman. My team made a successful planetfall but had to engage Chapman's hostiles using many android soldiers. Many friendlies are dead, all the invaders, I hope, but we successfully reclaimed the scientists. Over."

Ma continued, "The message is for the UAS base and Captain

Billings. Send medical help to Mortson2 for friendlies. Engage a business group to ensure friendlies have ample future supplies, food, water, etc., in trade for minerals. Finally, retrieve my team and the scientists to be returned to the nearest UAS base. Over."

"Message received. Can you stay on point for confirmation and return messages? Over." Gunnery Sgt. Alonus Wilson asked.

Ma thought through her options and replied, "No, Gunnie. I cannot. Without many details, I had to leave my team and find high ground to contact my lander to bounce the signal to you. Now, I need to regain my lander and move it to friendly territory. There, I can regain communication. Over?" Sgt. Ma finished.

"Well, you sound like you are up to your tits in biters. You do what you must, and we will leave the light on for you. Gunnery Wilson, over and out."

Ma thought, "Tits in biters? Leave the light on? I need to learn more Old Earth phrases and what they mean."

Ma turned back to Benzil and said, "You two find your way down to the meeting hall. Make sure Sgt. Grant knows who you are. Do not approach the place without calling out to him. Do you understand?"

Ma asked.

Benzil shook his head, grabbed his father's hand to pull him to his feet, but then asked, "What will you do, Sgt. Ma?"

Ma turned to him, "I have to get the lander and move it back to town. I can do it quickly without you two. That is the only way we can communicate with the UAS and protect the town and scientists. You two go now."

She watched them turn away with their remaining rations and water. She grabbed their restraints lying on the ground, tucked them and the communicator back into her pack, then turned in the lander's direction.

FOURTEEN

Auto Tripping

Sgt. Ma raised a lot of yellowish dust behind her big feet, running as fast as possible.

Even at her speed, it would be too much time to make the lander.

As things were desperate, she hoped she would not encounter any more obstacles.

When she made the lander, the sun was high overhead and went in through the open portal. She did not know how to operate this specific one, but she knew there was power in the lander's auto functions.

She planned to blast off and find 2000 meters automatically to get above the terrain, then move at speed horizontally in the direction she chose.

Once there, she would let the lander make planetfall, all the time hoping the fuel cells contained enough energy to go that far.

She strapped in and found the control panel. Rather than just touch buttons, she studied it and found there was a vocal command.

She tried it, "Lander, attention." Nothing happened. "Lander, respond."

She punched a button for information, and the electronic voice informed her in universal that the vocal had been disabled for security purposes.

She found the usefulness of one of Grant's words.

"Well, shit!"

She ran her fingers up the display panel and found one labeled "Auto."

"Dammit!" finding another Grant helpful word.

She punched Auto, and a small display screen came to life.

The display screen looked like she could execute what she wanted, but it would have to come as multiple commands, not the one she wanted.

First, Ma had to wake the ship.

Power on.

As she touched that button, lights came on, air whooshed, and her seat automatically conformed to her body.

She strapped herself in, chose the command for altitude, and punched in the 2000 meters to get her above the surrounding countryside and hills.

The rocket engines came on after a five-second countdown.

Boom, and she was going up.

Next, she chose the command for horizontal travel and punched in the compass directions she needed. The lander screen would have to serve as a locator.

The lander immediately began to speed along the autoroute.

Below her, she soon saw the trail the four had previously marched and quickly went over it.

There were gun placements below her. As the lander moved further, she saw the ridge through the display.

The town was just beyond it, so she executed a hover.

With a jolt, the lander came to a stop in mid-air.

Finally, she executed an auto descent, which probably would have been too fast for Grant, but she needed to get back there.

The lander dropped smoothly out of the sky and came within 10 meters of landing, slowing until it made planetfall.

Now, she executed the last command to put the lander back to sleep.

Power off.

The portal opened, and she ran out to check on her people.

FIFTEEN

Ma's Return

Sgt. Ma ran the three hundred meters from the lander to the edge of town. It was her first time piloting a ship, but she did not have time to think of it or congratulate herself.

Now, she was within fifty meters of the meeting hall, but she needed to be careful. She thumbed her radio three times but did not get a return from Sgt. Grant.

Had Grant passed out, or did something else happen?

She slowed her progress and then came in from the rear. She stepped up to one window and found the house was primarily empty of living souls. Sgt. Grant was lying on the floor, as were the three friendlies. The scientists were gone.

She ran around to the door and went directly to Grant, noting the friendlies all had holes in their heads, all three dead. It made her furious, but she had to control her emotions for now.

As soon as she reached him and rolled him over, she could see Grant had two shots to his chest, but he was still breathing. The wheezing sounds coming from his chest were not reassuring to her, though he held up his one unhurt hand to Ma and motioned for her to come close.

"Two came. Both shot me through the window, then shot the friendlies. I must have faded out. They left just a few minutes ago with the scientists."

Ma held his hand, wondering if there was a chance to save him. But Grant had other ideas.

“Ma, catch them, rip them apart, destroy them,” he hissed between his teeth.

The door opened, and Ma swung around to shoot whoever was there. It was Benzil and his father.

“Oh, no! We called out. No one answered. Are we too late?” Benzil asked.

Ma said, “Grab that first aid kit over there, and bring it here, quick.”

Benzil followed his orders and then bent down.

Ma grabbed the bandages, pushed some into Grant's bullet holes, and wound them around Sgt. Grant’s body. This action caused so much pain to him that Ma found tears on her cheeks. It startled her.

Why tears? She did not understand.

She wound the bandage tightly for several revolutions and lightly touched Grant’s shoulders where there were no wounds.

She grabbed Benzil and pulled him forward.

Benzil looked at her shoulders and realized she was bleeding.

“Sgt. You have been hit!”

Sgt. Ma felt where he was looking, and yes, she had been hit, then said, “I am ok for now, still functional. I think it was three shots, but they are in relatively safe places, and I believe they were all small caliber particles.”

“Stay with Grant. I have to go. Hold his hand, and give him sips of water. Please!” Ma begged.

SIXTEEN

Revenge

She was on her feet and running towards the Chapman lander as fast as she could. She should catch up with them, as they could not move quickly with their hostages.

She ran for about half a kilometer when she thought she saw them enter a tree line. She changed course by a degree and sped up her run. She reached the tree line and ran parallel to their route. In her head, she was trying to get ahead.

Then, suddenly, she had a new plan.

She would beat them to their lander.

Sgt. Ma made another slight course correction, and she felt she was close.

There was the end of the tree line, and she hid behind a large tree to sight the hill slightly to her left and then looked and listened back to her right for the hostiles.

She did not see them, but she could hear them. They were coming, but she felt she had the time to make it to their lander.

She burst forth from the trees, aimed for the hillside, and was up and over it in a flash.

Ma arrived at the lander and went inside. Though she knew little about spaceships, she knew how to make things break.

Firstly she had to find the fuel cells. When she did, she noted it used fixed nuts.

She screwed them out with her hands and pulled the protecting panel off.

Inside, she noted the connections and wondered which one was ground or return.

Any electrical circuit had to have a supply feeding energy out and a return as a complete circuit.

Sgt. Ma disconnected one wire, hoping it was the return, and broke its connector.

The engine would not start now.

Then, she went outside to hide behind the ship to see if she could attack them before they reached the troopship.

That could be very chancy since they used the Trionans as shields.

She saw there was no shot possible that would not risk the scientists.

The group made the lander, sending the scientists up the ramps with two men close behind.

Ma noticed the scientists seemed to be lurching as if their balance was poor.

The ramp quickly closed.

Sgt. Ma waited. There was no way the engine would start, and with some luck, neither of these two would know how to fix it.

After a short while, the ramp opened again, and one man descended. She could not tell if he was going back to town to get help or if he was looking for an android. He could start back up, hoping the android knew something.

Either way, Ma would eventually kill him. But the scientists had to be rescued again.

Ma found the nozzle for one engine nearest the ramp. She broke out her laser pistol, dialed back the power, and trained it on the pressure line. She followed the pressure lines back up into the ship with her eyes. Her idea was to make a tiny hole without blowing the damned thing up.

The first try did not work.

Sgt. Ma had to dial up more power.

This power setting was too much. A hole appeared on the near side of the pressure line but punched through the other side as well.

High-pitched squealing took place as the pressurized gas in the lines squeezed out through both holes.

There was no way the soldier in the ship could not hear the piercing whistle.

She waited under the ramp. Some seconds passed before his head came out to look left, then right.

Now he knew the source of the high-pitched scream. He came partway down the ramp, and turned to look back at the pressure line to get a better look. Ma grabbed his feet and jerked them backward. He fell directly onto his face.

Ma pulled him down to her, brought his face within an inch of hers, and she squeezed with her hands on either side of his face, holding him high enough where his feet did not reach the ground.

Sgt. Ma said, "You are brave man, killing unarmed civilians."

He struggled mightily, using his feet and hands to beat at her, but Ma would not let go.

He stupidly tried to grab her hands. She squeezed harder. His eyes bulged, and his mouth slavered drool. His feet slowed, and his mouth stopped shuddering just about the time his jaw broke. Ma would not stop. She pushed and pushed until his skull caved in.

Dead now and useless, she threw his body beneath the ramp and ran inside to the scientists.

Sgt. Ma knew that kill was unnecessarily brutal, but she did feel a little better killing him that way.

The friendlies in town had not deserved the attack.

As she approached the scientists, the group looked more drugged than afraid.

Ma bent down to them and tried to get their attention. Their responses were slow and disconnected.

She could carry two at a time, down the ramp and to some safe place, but it would take three trips to get all five. There was likely not enough time for that.

She looked around the ship and saw flexible sheet metal, likely used around an ammunition tray.

Now she looked for rope. She put the sheet metal on the ramp. Using the rope and starting from underneath the metal, she wrapped two pieces, one on the length, the other on the width, with plenty of slack left on both.

Next, she carefully put each scientist on the sheet metal. Then she crudely tied the ends together and ran a separate rope around each scientist.

In her way, she bound them to the sheet metal in a crudely made sled.

Now, she tied a final piece of rope to the long rope. This longer piece was so she could drag the metal and scientists down the ramp on her sled.

She had just begun when shots rang out from the tree line. It was the lone survivor walking with one android.

Likely this was a soldier switched off during the battle versus one she or Grant had shot. This android appeared undamaged.

They were still too far away to be useful, but that would change quickly.

Ma drug the scientists down the ramp as fast as she dared. She went around the spaceship to use it as cover and noticed a rock pile not very far away.

Within seconds, she had the scientists safely behind the rock pile. She thought this would be their stronghold but then remembered the missiles the android had.

She had to carry the battle to him, leaving the Trionans safe for now behind the rocks.

She ran back to the ship and drew a line of sight around it to the advancing android.

He was only one hundred meters away.

Sgt. Ma knew she would not get many shots before it launched missiles, so she pulled out her particle accelerator rifle and drew a careful bead on the android.

Headshots did not seem fruitful before, as she remembered the previous battle, where she hit them, and when they stopped soon. The spot where a human navel would be must be where the computer processing power was or perhaps the power source.

She had seen three androids stop in their tracks from the hostiles' initial attack when she hit it.

The android must have sensed her with infra-red and took a considerable leap, throwing her aim off. She would have to wait until it was on the ground again.

Her shot was perfect; the android went down.

Now, she could see the lone Chapman. She ran straight at him as he lowered his rifle, put it on full auto, and lay shots directly at her. A few hit her but did not change her velocity.

She hit him in his chest at full speed.

She had crushed his rib cage. She would not walk away from him yet.

As he lay below her, he whimpered. Ma leaned close and asked him, "All these innocent people you killed? Was it worth it?"

With that, Ma dug her middle finger into his chest wound, making him scream.

"You never answered me. Was it worth it?" Ma asked again while digging her finger in even deeper.

His screams became maniacal, and he thrashed, yet she dug.

Finally, she took the goo from his chest, broke open his mouth with enough power to break his jaw, and rubbed his chest cavity material onto his tongue with her finger as in his last moments.

She wanted to cause horror in him as he died.

He was still alive when she walked away, but she knew he would not live long.

She walked back to the scientists to see how they were doing. One was no longer behind the rock, as he had woken, heard the screams, and came to one side of the ship to see Ma brutalize the soldier.

He was silent as she walked up. But, when she stood over him, he said, "We Trionans have been peaceful for over a millennium. I know you had to protect us, but I'm not sure I can ever get this out of my memory."

"Sometimes, when one faces violence, one has to use violence to protect oneself or loved ones. Peace only happens after violence is met with greater violence!" she said.

She motioned for him to follow her back to the protective rock area.

The others were gaining consciousness.

She said, "Good. I see you are all coming out of whatever drug they forced upon you. Everyone Is safe now. I fear my partner is dead. We all need to go back to the meeting hall. Do you all feel up to the task?"

The lead Trionan said, "This ground does not give us pause. We cannot move at your speed, but we can cover much in a short time."

Ma said, “Ok, then. Let’s go. You set as fast a pace as you can manage, and I will keep up.”

The party of five Trionans ran down the ramp and moved out to the tree line. Their pace was slower than she would like, but it would take a few moments for the drugs to think faster.

SEVENTEEN

A Plan

The group ran with all due speed back to the blue meeting hall.

When Sgt. Ma entered the meeting hall, she expected the worst and went inside.

Benzil began, "Sgt. He is still alive. Though I can barely feel his pulse or watch his chest rise, he is breathing. I don't think he has long."

Benzil's father shook his head in mournful agreement and said something Ma took to be condolences.

Ma nodded and said, "I will try to get help as soon as possible, but no doubt it will take a while. I will go outside to begin communications with the lander."

She exited the meeting hall and keyed up her communicator to the lander. At this distance, it immediately responded, and she returned to the same frequency she was successful with.

She sent out the same identification communication stream as before, and the connection sound took place.

"Sgt. Ma? Gunnery Sgt. Good to hear from you. Wilson here. What is your status? Over."

Sgt. Ma began, "This situation has changed. In my aerial reconnaissance, I missed two hostiles. While I relocated the lander, they killed the three friendlies, recaptured the scientists, and shot my Sgt. twice in the chest. I reengaged with the enemy, killed both hostiles and one android, and reclaimed the scientists. But Sgt. Grant's pulse is feeble. He might not last very long. Over."

A new voice came online, "Sgt. Ma, this is Captain Billings. We have plotted the passage for you and can be there in 12 hours. This is our flank speed, so it will be the best we can do. Can you hang on till we get there? Over."

Sgt. Ma said, "Two concerns. Sgt. Grant will probably die, and whoever sent this ship from Chapman will probably try again. Ok, that would be midnight for me. I feel there is something more important here than I know right now. I am the last soldier standing. I will hold off the enemy as long as I can, and perhaps your team can save the Trionans that are left. Over."

There was a long pause with only space caused by radio static, and Captain Wilson asked, "Are there any final thoughts from you, then, Sgt. Ma of the UAS? Over."

Without a beat, Ma said, "No thoughts, no regrets. I am proud to serve the UAS. I lastly hope to get these scientists safe. Over and out."

And with that, she returned the communicator to her trail bag and went back inside.

"Look, there are several places replacement soldiers could land, and they will come straight here. I have an idea. Even though the lander is just a three-person craft, I think we can all fit in, thereby throwing out equipment we will not need. I can move it back up to the ridge. There are automatic gun placements we might use. Benzil, do you think you could get them operational again?"

Benzil immediately smiled and said, "Yes, I know where replacement drones are, and the guns were fine the last I saw them. There is plenty of ammunition up there as well."

Ma said, "Ok, you and your father grab whatever supplies you need up on that ridge and make as much speed as possible. If you have headlamps, you will probably need those. With the timing of this, it could be a nighttime fight. Your automatic gun placements will not care what light is available. I will try to get Grant and the scientists into the lander as safely as I can. I will try to meet you up there. The Chapmans will have to widen their search from here, but eventually, they will find us. If you find any of your town survivors, tell them to leave this place and go to the closest next town. Got it?"

Benzil shook his head and said, "Yes, I have it." He turned to his father and said a few words in his language, and the two left.

Ma turned back to the scientists and said, "If we live, we will have to work together; otherwise, we will all die. Can I depend on you?"

The one who always seemed to lead spoke up in his unmistakable voice, "We all understand. We will do whatever we can to help."

Ma said something, stopped, then tried again, "I don't even know your names, but we will have time for that later. I am not sure of the space we will have in the lander. Bring only yourselves, Grant's weapons, and field pack, and make your way to the lander. The ramp is down, and you go straight in. I will bring Grant, but I will have to move him gently and slowly. Start now."

The scientists gathered the gear she mentioned, immediately headed for the door, and turned in the lander's direction.

She knelt to put her arms beneath Grant and lifted him. With his added weight, she felt where she had been wounded. One was a stabbing pain in her back.

She made her way through the door and turned towards the lander.

She walked as smoothly but as quickly as she could.

She and Grant made the lander, went up the ramp, and saw all five scientists huddled together just outside. She lay Grant near them and ran into the lander.

She needed two of the flight chairs. The third one, she put her strength and weight to cause the fasteners on the floor to rip loose.

The chair was thrown out of the craft, leaving a half-meter tear in the flooring. Sgt. Ma threw everything else that was not necessary for the flight out of the vessel.

Two flight chairs were needed to hold herself and Grant.

"Ok, there is room. Please, all of you, board." Ma ordered.

She picked Grant up smoothly, almost lovingly, carried him into the ship to place him into his chair, and strapped him in.

Then she gained her oversized chair.

She woke the lander and again wondered how much fuel was still onboard.

Auto engagement and they rose to 2000 meters.

Auto horizontal, the lander moved while she watched the ground shift beneath her.

At the ridge, she slowed down the speed to a crawl.

When she saw the gun placement come into view, she glanced around for a safe place to land that was primarily flat but had less tree or rock cover.

There!

Auto descent and they were safely on the ground.

She put the lander back to sleep.

Again, she wondered how much fuel was left in the fuel cells. She glanced at the display panel and noticed one button that might give her the answer.

"Supply"

She punched it, and the red flashing warning told her everything. There was not enough left for a lift-off. The lander was now useless to her but had performed necessary functions to get them this far.

"Ok, you, Trionans. Travel up the slope and find the gun placement. I will follow up with Grant. While you are up there, look for a small hole that leads to a cave. Explore it. See if you can all get into it. I will see you there." Ma finished and turned to retrieve Grant from his restraints.

She heard the scientists leave and walked gently down the ramp, holding Grant like a newborn baby.

While moving up the slope, she was pleased the Trionans had found the gun and the cave.

The leader spoke beautifully clearly, "We surveyed the cave. It is more than big enough for all of us. And, to make introductions, I am or was the Survey Commander. We shortened our names to make it easier for you, as they have quite a few syllables. You can call me Sisn. That handsome guy to your left is Pickna, to his left is Koung, behind me is Reslie, and to my left is Blempis. That should do for now. But, for brevity, just refer to Sisn, and I will make sure the others do as you need."

Ma almost smiled, "Thank you. Thank you all. If I give you the sign, you all pile into that cave as quickly as possible. Is there room for Grant? I feel I should put him down and not move him again, and I need him safe so I can fight."

Survey Commander Sisn said, "Yes, there is more than enough room inside. But I am afraid you cannot make it inside. There is an indentation to the left of the entrance. Perhaps two of us go inside, and you hand him to us?"

Ma said, "Agreed."

As she watched, Sisn flagged one other, whom she thought was Pickna, and they went inside.

She approached, knelt, and placed Grant into their waiting tentacles. They gently lowered him to the ground.

Now, she had to recon the hillside to see the weaknesses and hope Benzil could make it sooner than later.

This location was high ground, so any ground troops approaching would have to climb. Sgt. Ma felt the most likely attack point was in line with the town, so she moved two guns over there.

But they could also attack from the sky, so the remaining gun would have to have 360 degrees of kill with angling for shooting up and not out.

She set it all to automatic, letting the sensors and drone find the targets. She did not know how to perform checks on them to ensure they were fully operational. Benzil would be necessary for that.

Sgt. Ma would stay behind rock cover to last as long as possible when the attack came.

Satisfied, she knew her kill zones and defensive weaknesses; she went back to the cave to check on Grant.

Sisn was by his side but strangely had removed his gauze and bandage.

"Sisn. Is that wise? You are exposing his wounds to whatever is out here, germs, dust, but also encouraging a bleed out." Ma said.

Sisn said, "A little faith, please. Long ago, we accidentally found our saliva could kill common germs and, with carbon-based animals, could encourage skin cells to grow. The wounds Grant has been mostly through and through. There is only one where a particle might still be inside. So, this is worth the risk. I will try to sterilize each location with my saliva and hope each location grows over, preventing more blood loss. He is so close to death. I felt it was worth the risk."

Ma quickly considered everything he said and responded, "Go ahead. Your words are the best news I have heard."

Ma stayed a few more minutes to watch. Sisn's mouth was underneath his body, so he stood over Grant and let his drool hit the wounds. Ma found it fascinating how accurate he was.

But then she went back out to find a location to use her field glasses to sight in on the town. She could likely see a ship land from this distance and count how many soldiers were coming out of it.

EIGHTEEN

Ready to Fight

Sisn came out and asked her if he could assist and said, "I believe I have done all I can for Grant. He is still alive. His pulse is weak but stable."

Ma said, "That is good. I hope he makes it. I do not know how far Chapman's planet is or how quickly they can supply more soldiers, but we should have a few hours to rest. Neither Grant nor I took the time to study this solar system, but only this planet. You and I must hold this ground for another ten hours. I hope to see Benzil soon. Otherwise, it will not be much of a standoff."

Sisn nodded and went back to the cave.

Sgt. Ma spoke to his back and said, "Make sure everyone gets some rations and water. We will probably need it."

Ma broke out her field glasses and thought to look for Benzil and his father. She could see them, but they appeared to be at least an hour away.

She could do nothing but wait, so she broke out her rations and water and settled down to rest.

Only one of her wounds bothered her: the one on her back. She could feel something in there if she strained the right muscle or leaned against a rock. She was not dizzy and felt ok. Therefore her blood loss must be minimal. She allowed herself time to close her eyes and just recoup. Her other wounds must have already clotted, as none of them she could see were bleeding.

Later, Benzil and his father arrived carrying three field packs. They had brought five drones but additionally more ammunition and food.

She bounced up when she heard them scrabbling up the hill.

Benzil waved at her and smiled, and said something to his father.

They gained the top and briefed Ma. Benzil said, "Sgt. These drones can stay aloft for 2 hours, but that is it. We have no way of recharging them. I did not think we needed more ammunition, but I brought spares anyway. Let me get to the control circuits and do a few tests to ensure the computers are still functional. I will first put the drones on maneuvers, just for a minute or so, to make all cameras work and the guns are following correctly. Then I will shoot one round from each. Does that sound ok to you?"

Sgt. Ma said, "Sure. These are yours, except for the test round. We cannot risk it. You make them work."

"That is ok. The test-firing will be virtual, and minimal sound will take place. It will just fire a small-caliber projectile.

Benzil piddled with this assembly or that one and finally turned on the computers. Electronically, it was functioning. On the ground, he could test various sensors by walking around them.

Now, he gave the order for all five drones to lift off. Yellowish clouds marked each lift-off. He seemed satisfied as they flew around according to his commands. He said, "The electronics are perfect."

He turned it on for the sky gun and asked the sensor to track flying objects short-range, then threw a rock up and past the firearm. One shot hit the rock.

Benzil said, "All functions are in the green. Have you checked your weaponry?"

Ma smiled at him and said, "I have been a soldier for a long time. Whenever I am not firing a weapon, I check them before firing. I am locked and loaded with a full magazine on each. All charge levels are in the green."

"Now we wait and hope the UAS ship gets here, and the Chapman ship never does. Everyone rest," Ma said.

The afternoon was speeding past when she estimated it must be near six.

They heard rather than saw a ship coming into the atmosphere with a boom.

Sisn and his group came out to see what the clamor was.

Sgt. Ma looked at him and asked, "Do you know of any reason Chapman would risk so many resources to get the five of you? I can logically understand one troop carrier looking for you, but two? And I don't think this was a simple hostage-taking, as the Chapman soldiers destroyed everything in sight. There has to be more to this."

Sisn glanced at his people and said, "Maybe it is for element 115? Do you know? Star Fuel. We found very high concentrates here. It is unique in that it is not stable at all in nature. We all thought it was highly unusual to find a stable supply of it, and we theorized that something in the soil surrounding the 115 was the cause. It is locked in a unique ore. Mortson2 is ultra-valuable in this way. All supplies we know of need a tedious and costly process to extract 115."

Ma nodded, considered, and then said, "That does make more sense. They had to kill the locals because the locals knew of you. They had to capture you because you know of the ore and how to extract it. But how did they know of the existence of the element?"

Sisn seemed to hang his head, "Well, we were excited, and as peaceful scientists, we do not think of bad people in the world. We had an exciting discovery, so we reported it in the clear, no encryption."

Ma suddenly had all the pieces.

She got back on her communication device quickly, recorded a message, and did not wait for the UAS ship Tesla to connect with her encryption. She let the auto function do that for her.

She recorded all she knew, explained the ore and value, and suggested to Captain Billings that the UAS needed to send more troops to protect the entire planet from looters for all good. She had battled one pirate, and would likely have another today, but more would be on the way from other worlds.

She saw the ship come in through her field glasses and find a landing place. She did not know what to expect. More androids, more killers.

The portal opened two minutes after landing, but no soldiers came out. She could not see little drones from this distance but just imagined drones would be the eyes and likely the ears for the ground team.

Five more minutes passed, the portal closed up, and the ship lurched back into the air. It seemed to track something the drones followed, and the drones followed their path.

“Ok, they are coming. Get ready to fight. Benzil and your father behind those rocks,” Ma ordered.

Ma took her guns off the safety and found a rock cover for herself.

She was more than ready to fight.

NINETEEN

Battle Lines

The ship got within a few klicks and found a landing place.

Sgt. Ma thought to herself, "Good, we have a chance with a land battle. They would have obliterated us from the sky but might have killed the scientists."

She knew they would send drones to see how strong her position was and know where the scientists were.

The first drone she saw was far away and going in the wrong direction. She let it. No use helping them find where they huddled.

The second drone was further off course from the first one, but the third drone would pass over their position.

She drew a bead on it and at fifty meters, used one shot to take it down. It would have seen them hiding behind the rocks with infrared sensors.

Now the pirates knew where they were.

Shooting down one drone caused the other two drones to head for her position. One came from her right, while the second one led in from the left. Both could likely use telemetry to 3D map the location.

She knew troops must now come up with the slopes. The auto gun placements would see them first and begin to fire at 30 meters.

Benzil was located nearby. He and his father would re-ammo the units when they ran out. Both would be exposed for the 15 seconds necessary to do this.

Ma would not fire until they made the plateau, but the soldiers would likely have gone right and left to avoid the gun placements.

The gun placement to the left took its first shot. It was programmed to spit one bullet at a time until a mass charge of soldiers took place.

Ma heard the splat of the bullet and a grunt. That was a living soldier, not an android, from the sound of the shell hitting its target.

Then, the gun placement on the right shot once, and it too caused a splat with a cry. That was a living soldier.

The guns sped up left and right, firing more shells, showing there were multiple targets. The gun on the left spun off-axis, more to the left, and spit more bullets in that direction, while the gun on the right also moved its axis left and shot more.

Two minutes later, they both reversed.

Ma thought the soldiers were taking evasive action climbing the hill, trying to find a weakness.

She was at the ready, but the guns went silent, indicating the soldiers had stopped. Likely, they were regrouping to figure another attack plan out. And, if she was lucky, there were at least two of their number dead.

Ma got Benzil's attention, moving her hand from an eye to a palm. She wanted to know what he saw on the cameras.

He nodded and held up both hands. He folded one. So, fifteen more soldiers?

The guns were quiet, and Ma realized grenades were likely next. She motioned to Benzil and his father to get low and motioned with her hands as if someone was lobbing a grenade.

It began with one, but soon there was a flurry. Grenades

exploded over the plains, throwing large yellowish clouds into the air.

Shrapnel hit the rocks she and Benzil hid behind, but none found them. Even though the soil was falling over Benzil and his father, Benzil was watching the cameras. With his hands, he indicated to Ma, "They are coming."

The guns started firing again, faster and faster, with more splats and grenades. When the first three made the plateau, they ran the ridgeline to Ma's left.

She shot the first two, and as they fell, the third dropped to a prone firing position to return fire on her. The bullets bounced around the rock in a ricochet manner. She had to duck as several rock shards caught various body parts.

Sgt. Ma looked at Benzil and noticed he had superficial cuts to his face and hands. His eyes were locked onto his firing screens.

Then, she noticed that two more attackers had made it to the plateau on her right and lobbed grenades. They were too far away to be effective, and she shot one quickly.

It was a lung shot; he went down but still alive. Ma knew he would not survive for as long as he would drown in his blood.

Both left and right gained another soldier, and the bullets increased on their mark, Sgt. Ma. The auto gun placements had slowed down, and Benzil would have to retrain them to the two ridgelines.

All hell was breaking loose in front of Ma. She was startled when a shot went off behind her, then another. She took a second to glance, and there was Grant, prone just outside the cave but doing his best to return hellfire. He got one on the right and forced the other behind the kill zone to retreat.

Ma could not believe it but decided to let Grant have that position as she needed him.

Sgt. Ma moved out from behind her rock to charge the ridgeline on the left. The soldiers were held down by Grant and never dreamed Ma would charge.

One soldier saw this substantial dark being running towards them through a hail of gunfire and decided to run. Ma shot him in the back and sped up.

She was within striking distance when one of the other soldiers shifted his attention away from Grant, saw Ma, and tried to shoot her. It was too late.

She grabbed his gun with one hand and lifted him to shield herself from the remaining hostile.

That hostile lifted his full auto gun and emptied it into his soldier mate.

Ma reached under her lifted soldier's left armpit with one hand and shot the hostile between his eyes.

The one in her arms tried to struggle, but she broke his neck with one hand and threw him over the ridge with the other.

Sgt. Ma stopped.

It was quiet.

The dead soldier flying over the rock and ridgeline caused some to react.

A gentle breeze swept in front of her face, momentarily giving her respite. On the draft, she knew she smelled man-fear.

Were they safe?

She had made into tree cover to hide but immediately moved to the hillside to see any hostiles still climbing.

She kept moving till she could see the ship. Along her path, she saw no other soldiers that were alive but plenty of bodies.

The ship portal was closed. What did that mean?

She ran back to the plateau to check on her charges. Benzil and his father were reloading the guns. Sisn was kneeling beside Sgt. Grant.

"He is out but still has a pulse. I could not stop him. Once he heard the gunfire, he was coming to your aid. He pointed his gun at me and told me to sit down." Sisn said while shaking his head. "I tried to keep him alive. I don't know if he can make it."

Sgt. Ma shook her head, "I understand. Let's get him back inside. I am afraid the next portion will be an aerial battle. Let me hand Grant to you. Benzil, you and your father as well. Go as deep into the cave as you can. Benzil, you take my laser pistol, and Sgt. Grant's. Put the scientists behind you and try to shoot anyone other than me. Got it?"

She opened her mouth to say something else but was interrupted by the sky gun tracking something. She went back to her rock cover.

Sgt. Ma did not need field glasses to see this; the enemy lander came in hot and heavy. It seemed to be on a suicide mission, pointed straight at her rock-shaded position while the sky gun went full automatic.

Ma thought she had one shot before the ship hit. She aimed for space just above and behind where the engines were. This fuel tank was likely filled with element 115, a volatile fuel.

Her shot hit, and the explosion took out the ship.

A pressure wave and an orange-red fireball swept towards her. It lifted her above the countryside and threw her like a rag doll.

Fiery debris rained down on the plateau area, and larger pieces fell and made the ground tremble.

Ma's world went black with no worries, pain, or enemies.

TWENTY

Rescue

Sgt. Ma was first aware of the blinding light and the pain in her shoulders.

She could not feel anything lower than her waist.

She tried to put her hand over her eyes, but the hand felt strange.

Ma opened her eyes and looked at what must be a cast over her hand, extending down her wrist almost to the elbow. Her eyes glanced down as far as they could see, and everywhere there appeared to be medical coverings, tubes, and wires, making her body look like a wild science experiment.

There were various swishing sounds and beeps around her from the medical equipment.

For a moment, she felt she was outside of her body, as this was not hers.

Someone came from her right and said softly, "Sgt. Ma, you are safe. I am Doctor Thorton. We have assessed your wounds, and bound them where we could. There is one fragment in your back near your spine. The ship exploded and threw you up from what we gathered, and you landed 10 meters away. The particle was driven deeper into your back when you fell, and now it is lodged in a spinal disc. We don't have the medical equipment necessary to remove it, so you are on a back brace to protect your spinal column from movement. If it moves anymore, you might not walk again. Please be calm."

Ma thought all this through, shook her head, and asked, "What about Sgt. Grant and the Trionans? What about Benzil and his father?"

Dr. Thorton patted her shoulder and said, "All are ok because of you. Except for Sgt. Grant. We have him on life support. He is one heartbeat above the dead. Your Trionan Sisn saved his life, but Grant almost threw that work away, coming to your defense. I feel he has a 20% chance to live, though I cannot say he will be a functional soldier again. Do you feel like talking more? Our gunnery Sgt. and Captain is dying to meet you?"

"Yes, of course. I would like to meet them as well." Ma said.

She could hear the Doctor walking away, a door opened, and she heard two more people coming in, though she could not move enough to see them.

She had to wait until they were almost over her.

"Hi, Sarge. Don't move. I am Captain Billings." Captain Billings said and saw Ma was trying to salute, her arm and hand moving towards her brow.

"Dammit, soldier, at ease. Our Dr. here is damned good, but you cannot move now if you ever want to soldier again."

Ma knew she was beaten, "Yes, sir. No more movement from me."

Another voice spoke up. Ma knew it instantly.

"Sarge, Gunnery Sgt. Wilson here. I am so honored to meet you. Once we understood the situation, especially when we found you, it was a wonder you lived. The war zone, hell, the war zones on that planet showed heavy destruction and loss of life. It is amazing to us anyone lived."

Captain Billings spoke again, "Sgt. Ma that goes double for me. You and Grant did an outstanding job against overwhelming battle conditions. From the people you were protecting, I am astounded by your battlefield situational awareness and insight."

Ma shook her head and said, "I was doing my job."

Captain Billings said, "Bullshit! One normal soldier would have asked for evac when they encountered the first ship of hostiles, let alone the second. We have interviewed the Trionans and agree with your analysis. We contacted UAS Brigade headquarters, and they are dispatching a battalion to take control of Mortson2. Survey Commander Sisn has offered his services as well. We can chase the pirates back to Chapman and prosecute whoever funded and oversaw this mess. I have recommended the death penalty for the person or persons involved. There is a fat cat hidden away from the fight. The UAS will find them to prosecute."

Gunnery Sgt. Wilson glanced at the Captain and vigorously motioned to Ma, using one hand fingers out to demonstrate.

Billings said, "Well, Sgt. Wilson, you are so damned eager, you tell her." But he smiled when he said it.

Sgt. Wilson bent over Ma and whispered to her, "We have been in contact with your Colonel Haskell on Crageor3. He knows everything we know. He got your Major General Harris involved. We must transfer you over to a UAS starship, but both the Colonel and Major General will be there to greet both you and Grant when you arrive on Crageor3. For God's sake, do not salute them. You will both get field commendations for Valor and a new stripe. You should be proud. You both earned it. I think the Major General has a special treat for you. It sounds like you might be in front of the camera for a while. You know, till your body heals." Gunnery Sgt. Wilson was smiling from ear to ear. He gently grabbed her unharmed left hand and squeezed.

Captain Billings and Gunnery Sgt. Wilson looked at each other, and the Captain called out, "Attention."

Their right heels contacted their left heels with a slap as their hands snapped to their brows in a military salute.

Sgt. Ma had just received the most honorable compliment in her life. Tears were now streaming down her face.

She shook her head and started to speak, but Captain Billings put a hand over her mouth and said, "I know you were just doing your job. The best job the two of us have ever heard of a soldier doing under these conditions. Those scientists you saved are hugely important for star travel, and their discoveries will benefit all of us."

He went back to attention and said smartly, "Sgt. Ma of the All Worlds United Armed Services, I order you to be at ease and follow every doctor's commands. We want you healthy and back at war when you are able. Do you understand, Sgt. Ma?"

Ma was having so much trouble processing this that she could not stop the tears. She shuddered when she answered, "Yes, Captain, I understand. You must forgive me. On my homeworld, tears are unusual. I don't know how to turn them off."

The Captain and Sergeant were two proud soldiers leaving the room, clapping each other on the shoulder.

They were proud of what they had witnessed and who they had met. They would repeat this war story to anyone sitting still long enough to hear it.

The door closed softly behind them.

Dr. Thorton came back into her view. "You and I will spend the next three weeks together until we can reach the starship for transfer. The Captain and Gunnery Sgt. will go into hibernation. I must stay awake to tend to you and your partner, Sgt. Grant. By the by, the boy named Benzil said he thought you and Grant did not go together, but he recounted how Grant stood up in every situation to fight by your side. Even when Grant should have been dead, he crawled to fight with you. Without a doubt, you make one helluva team!"

Sgt. Ma said, "Grant is a fine soldier and braver than anyone I have ever seen. If that part is not in the field report, I will add it."

Dr. Thorton said, "I don't think you have to worry about that. You two were marvelous. Someone will write a song about this. Hell, I bet televids will be created. By the by, Benzil said he wanted to enlist in the UAS, hoping he could fight along your side."

Sgt. Ma smiled through her tears with that comment.

Dr. Thorton went back to his computers, watching her vitals while Ma lay there, breathing, crying, and remembering the recent battles, reliving the missiles, grenades, bullets, and the enemy.

In particular, she said to no one, "I am a soldier. I was doing my job, dammit!"

Another thought passed into a question, "Why did the Captain say Bullshit?"

TWENTY-ONE

Colonel Haskell

Colonel Haskell waited in his office for the arrival of two soldiers. The ones he had seen carried off the UAS ship six months ago and could not believe either was alive would arrive soon.

He was as nervous as he had been when he was 12 and tried his first kiss with a girl named Shelly. She had buck teeth but had recently gained some hardware that would eventually tame her dentures.

He was Bobby at that time and was petrified. He remembered that his mind seemed frozen, as his hands and knees were shaking. Shelly made a move towards him, he towards her, and awkwardly their lips finally touched.

Why was he nervous? Why in the hell did he remember that first kiss?

"Dammit, breathe, man. This is not the first time you sent soldiers into harm's way. They came back shot up, but these two did come back."

He had not been this excited in a very long time as he remembered the first time the two of them met in his office and heard the bravado of little Freddie go quiet when Sgt. Ma entered. He remembered Sgt. Grant pissing his pants.

He laughed a little. He remembered when he sent them off, worried both might not return.

Then he remembered the motorized gurneys coming out of the ship. He could still see all the wires and tubes on those gurneys. He could easily remember that Sgt. Grant was just above the dead, and Ma barely one step better.

When seeing Major General Harris and himself, Ma had tried to salute with several wires, tubes, and casting on her arm.

Both he and General Harris were stunned, but Harris came to her senses first.

"At ease, soldier. Rest that arm. We have been briefed on your spine."

Sgt. Ma, "Yes, General," as tears leaped to her eyes. Ma felt ashamed she could not show proper military manners.

The officers went to each soldier and pressed their healthy hands out of respect.

Grant never felt it, Sgt. Ma did.

Major General Harris quietly said, "Sgt. You will rest. You will heal. You will have any path you choose. So will Sgt. Grant. But not today. Today is a journey you will have to walk to heal, to see how much of your body is left to you and what you want to do with it! In a while, you and I will talk again about your future in the UAS."

Colonel Haskell bent over Sgt. Ma spoke quietly, "Damn, you two are soldiers any officer can be proud of. The UAS is proud of you. And that planet will help all of us, eventually."

So now he waited, as nervous as a cat, waiting for those two to enter his office again.

He had another severe case in front of him, and out of all the soldiers in his command, he knew there was one choice. But this time, he had to let them talk, see how they felt, and see if they were ready.

The door opened, Sgt. Grant came in first, followed by Sgt. Ma. They had new ribbons on their chest and a new stripe.

They came to attention.

Their right heel connected with their left as both hands snapped to their brow, one giant soldier and one small one.

Colonel Haskell looked into their eyes and only saw the determination of warriors.

He knew what the answer to his questions would be.

"Are you ready for more Hell? Are you ready to soldier?"

Made in the USA
Middletown, DE
26 August 2022

72355932R00083